A Dangerous Obsession

Alice Frank

Alice Frank

A Dangerous Obsession

MEMOIRS

Cirencester

Published by Memoirs

MEMOIRS
PUBLISHING

Memoirs Books

25 Market Place, Cirencester, Gloucestershire, GL7 2NX
info@memoirsbooks.co.uk   www.memoirspublishing.com

Copyright ©Alice Frank, March 2012

www.facebook.com/alicefrankauthor
Twitter: @Author_Alice

First published in England, March 2012

ISBN 978-1-908223-78-4

Printed in England

Contents

Introduction

Chapter 1	Footprints in the woods	Page 1
Chapter 2	The mind of Paul Stalker	Page 17
Chapter 3	Mrs Bent's obsession	Page 29
Chapter 4	Sisley gets to work	Page 39
Chapter 5	Looping	Page 56
Chapter 6	Red tape	Page 70
Chapter 7	Sanity and delusions	Page 89
Chapter 8	Lodger trouble	Page 101
Chapter 9	Escape	Page 114
Chapter 10	Endings	Page 128
	Postscript	Page 135

INTRODUCTION

This book is based on a true story. It tells what happened to an ordinary woman called Elizabeth Elders and her mother because of the actions of two sick and perverted people; a greedy, vindictive, woman-hating relative and a jealous, out-of-control social worker. Over a period of two years, Elizabeth and Rose Elders were hounded, bullied and intimidated almost to the point of madness, all because certain junior public servants misused their power, while senior ones who could have stopped it failed to use theirs properly.

The story recalls the terrible case of the multiple murderer Dr Harold Shipman, who targeted not the weak and dying but healthy people who were living full lives. As in that case, Elizabeth and Rose Elders were the victims of someone in authority who was jealous or resentful of someone who had nothing wrong with them.

I believe this story shows how open to abuse the 1983 Mental Health Act is (now the 2007 Mental Health Act). It allows social workers to do almost anything, as long as they can claim that it is 'in the interests of the patient'.

When I was working on the final draft of this book I was optimistic that I would be able to say now, in 2012, that mental health legislation has been amended to state that if a mental health team are going to act upon a complaint about a patient, they have to try to investigate it. I'm afraid this has not happened. The Department of Health have confirmed this for me. They have written in a letter to me, "*Any proposal to make an amendment now would be subject to parliamentary scrutiny, could only be brought forward when parliamentary timetable allowed and there is competing demand for parliamentary time.*"

This depressed me for a while, and then I found that there still may be hope, or at least that there may be some improvement in the next four to five years. All Acts of Parliament are constantly under review. The charities working in mental health are looking for ways to improve it, and most of them have a lawyer working for them. They may be able to achieve the condition that opinions should if possible be based on evidence which is known to be factual, and not on hearsay that may be false or mistaken.

I can't get officials to answer the question, 'Will you put it into the Mental Health Act that opinions should be based on correct facts?' They seem unable to understand the question.

The Department of Health said that the Act makes provision for a number of safeguards. One of them is that *"less restrictive alternatives must be considered before deciding on and making the application for the patient to be admitted into hospital under a section of The Mental Health Act."*

That's no safeguard against information being made up. It means they can still accept and act upon false allegations and refuse to investigate them. Let's compare it with what happens in the criminal justice system. Imagine a man is accused of shoplifting. The courts would say, "He denies stealing the television set. He says he's got an alibi that shows he was somewhere else at the time. Let's listen to the witnesses before we decide if he's guilty and should be punished". They would not say, "We won't send him to prison, we'll use a less restrictive alternative".

I remember coming back from France on the ferry and going through customs. I was told what a lot of power the custom officers had, but I still felt safe because the system isn't open to abuse. For example, they can't say you're smuggling cigarettes in your suitcase without having a look. They have to see the cigarettes. You can't get into trouble just because the customs men think you look like a smuggler – they have to prove it, otherwise you are free to go on your way.

People contact me to say how upset they are at being labelled as mentally ill. "They are telling lies about me!" they cry down the phone to me. People get very frightened when they have it explained to them that if the mental health team refuse to investigate a complaint about them they will have to accept that they've been sectioned and be forcibly held pending an appeal which can take as long as 28 days. A lot of damage can be done in that time.

If a patient complains about a social worker, the mental health team don't have to get the complaint right. They can say, "This patient is saying we've been breaking her windows" when the complaint is quite different. They can still act upon it regardless, and there is no simple or straightforward way of stopping them. If they are going to explain the complaints procedure to a patient, they should inform them at the same time about The Harassment Act 1997 and The Human Rights Act.

I also hear how social workers will say to parents, "You complain about us and we'll take away your children."

In cases of domestic violence a man who wants control will sometimes seek the support of the mental health team. Sometimes they get it, as happened in the case in this book. This can be due to lack of training, though it was not so in this case. A social worker is not qualified to make a diagnosis of mental illness – it is not in their training. You have to take care when calling a patient a thief, especially when writing it in their notes, but that's common knowledge, not lack of training. And only a judge can decide when libel has been committed.

It is not lack of training that made the social worker fail to realise that the old lady's nephew was simply after her money, even though he was phoning everyone up and blatantly asking questions about her financial affairs. It's common sense. However, a psychologist giving evidence in court who said the problem was perhaps that she felt inadequate and wanted control and it was transference of guilt, or she had a bad father or mother, would be challenged about it, and asked, "Are you sure its not lack of training?"

People transfer guilt when they are in denial of their own faults and want to put them on someone else. They live in fear of their own weaknesses being discovered and the less they understand themselves, the more they do it. They cover up their own behaviour by accusing other people.

I believe that homosexuals, or even men who have merely been accused of homosexuality, can be victims of this. I am referring to these cases where the police try to catch homosexual men out by looking at them through a spyhole. One man said that he had not done such a thing and wasn't even a homosexual, but he pleaded guilty. I can understand that. A lot of people would say they would never plead guilty if they were innocent, but how do they know that if they have never been in that situation? They don't know how daunting these authorities can be - how they can push you to doing anything. I find it quite worrying that psychologists reckon that some of these people who are so hard on homosexuals have a guilty conscience and secretly fear that they may be homosexual themselves.

The ministers were refusing to put it into the Mental Health Act that if social workers are going to enforce their opinions they must base their actions on facts, not unproven allegations.

It was 1992 when Elizabeth first started being persecuted by her cousin, and 1993 when he gained the support of Social Services. That was when her real problems began. In 1994 Elizabeth began to campaign for change to mental health legislation to ensure that social workers have to investigate allegations which may be spurious. They cannot just take the self-proclaimed victim's word for what happened. When the latest Mental Health Act came out in 2007 without addressing the problem it seemed the battle had been lost, but there is hope of change in the future.

A misogynist, a man who hates women, may use allegations about a pet to gain control of his victim. This is something that the RSPCA are very experienced in. He may phone them up and say the woman is ill-treating her dog or cat. Yet I have never heard it's not safe for that woman to let the RSPCA into the house and have a look at the pet to see if the claims are true. It is not like letting social workers in. Once they've seen you face to face the power they have is far more open to abuse.

I believe a lot of people confuse the Mental Health Act and its powers to detain people with those of the police. They don't realise that these come under completely different legislation. For example, people are more protected from being arrested on grounds of suspicion. If a woman accuses a man of rape, the police can only detain someone for up to 24 hours without either charging or releasing him unless an officer with the rank of superintendent or above, or magistrates, give permission for an extension. At the end of that time the suspect is released unless evidence has been found to charge them.

I have known patients left in a mental hospital while staff go away over a bank holiday, with another two weeks to wait before a tribunal comes round. When the staff come back from their holiday they may then decide to investigate it, find out the patient is innocent and let him or her out. The police would never get away with any of that. But the key difference is that the police cannot justify detaining someone by saying it is in their own interests.

I know someone who has recently been refused counselling simply because she won't tell them who her doctor is.

Psychologists find it very interesting that when Dr Harold Shipman was killing his elderly patients it wasn't the severely ill ones, the ones in a vegetative state, he was killing - it was the ones who were living full lives, doing useful charity work. It was the same with Elizabeth and her mother. When a social worker was trying to take over their lives for them it wasn't when they needed her. It was when they were looking after themselves perfectly well and going out every day to do charity work. They would go to bed early in order to get up early the next morning and start again.

But this is a story about malpractice, not general practice. We all know there are many very good social workers and doctors, as well as a few rogues and deranged ones. Normally, when a man has a nervous breakdown, he is bewildered by his private hell; he can no longer manage the simplest things, things he previously could do every day with no problem at all. A lot needs explaining to him. It is normal practice for a social worker to go round to his house and gently explain that he is having a nervous breakdown. It can be all his problems in a nutshell. But in certain kinds of malpractice, a social worker or clinician does not want the patient to get better; he or she wants to control them. It may be rare, but it happens. This is what this book is about.

Last night I dreamed that I jumped into some water with my dog. I assumed he could swim, but he couldn't. I fought desperately to keep him above the water, but he was too heavy. He sank beneath it more times than I could count and for longer than it would be possible to keep him alive. Yet he survived, for although I too was frequently beneath the water, we managed to swim to the side together and get out. It was in the country and no one was about. We climbed up a hill together and found a school at the top. I looked through the window and in it was a class full of schoolchildren. I thought, "It would have been all right, they'd have been able to get us both out of the water."

I have no doubt what this dream meant. No matter how much you think you've lost a thing, never give up. The dog may be at the bottom of the pond, but the school is at the top of the hill. Don't lose hope.

Chapter One

FOOTPRINTS IN THE WOODS

At the time this story begins, Rose Elders and her daughter Elizabeth were working for a charity in a Victorian mansion called The Towers, out in the country. The house was surrounded by trees and on dark evenings the atmosphere often became sinister and threatening.

Elizabeth would often work until nine or ten o'clock at night. At night it was an eerie, spooky place to be left alone. Except that one night, it became clear that she was not alone.

It was late one winter's evening and she was walking home down the lonely footpath with a girl when she spotted the figure of a man in the trees. 'Is that a fox?' said the girl. Elizabeth knew it was not a fox, but she was afraid to tell her. Elizabeth was vulnerable and for a long time she had been greatly intimidated.

Elizabeth thought she recognised the man as her cousin, Paul Stalker, but she didn't dare to say anything that could be interpreted as paranoia, for that would be dangerous; there was a social worker who had it in for her. Social workers can have a lot of power.

Elizabeth knew the man had expected her to be alone. He had intended to appear suddenly to terrify her, then deny he had ever been there. When she complained about it, he would say she was paranoid.

The next day she found footprints on the spot where he had been standing, and took a witness to look at them with her so they couldn't say she was making it up. They not only saw where he had been but where he had jumped over a fence and walked through a field to get to the spot.

There seemed little point in taking it any further. There was nothing in the Mental Health Act 1983 to say that anyone had to investigate such a thing, and the more she talked about what evidence she had the more it was used as evidence that she was paranoid.

* * * * * * * * * *

Paul Stalker was determined to get his hands on his Aunt Rose's money. Mrs Elders lived in a big house in the nearby town of Grimley and she had money. The only thing that was stopping Stalker from getting his hands on it was Elizabeth. She and her mother were very close to one another and he felt certain she would leave it all to her. So he had worked out a plot. He would get Elizabeth put into a mental hospital, and then, once she was out of the way, he would be able to take control of Mrs Elders and persuade this frail old lady to leave it all to him instead.

Stalker was optimistic that his plan would work. He knew that years before Elizabeth had already had one nervous breakdown; surely it wouldn't take much to drive her to another and get her put away.

He started by making a phone call to the Mental Health Department of Social Services. He told them a very big lie. He said he had been inside the house and seen Elizabeth being aggressive towards her mother. She had behaved like a madwoman, he said, and Mrs Elders had been terrified. He said he was afraid Elizabeth would hurt her.

An Approved Social Worker (the official title for a social worker in mental health) came round to the house to talk to them about it. Her name was Marjorie Bent. Mrs Bent did not realise that she was dealing with a routine case of a vulnerable person being exploited. It was strange that she did not see that Stalker merely wanted their support in getting control.

In fact, it was strange that Mrs Bent had ever been allowed to do this job at all. It had sometimes been wondered if her previous employers had given her a good reference just to get her out of their department.

Mrs Bent did not tell Elizabeth that she had come to see her as a psychiatric patient, and that she specialised in mental health. Nor did she tell her that she had received a phone call from Paul Stalker and it was this that had prompted her to come. Mrs Elders had been going to a club for old people and had been talking about Stalker there. She assumed that this was how Mrs Bent had first heard of them.

Elizabeth thought she was being interviewed simply as the nearest relative of someone elderly and vulnerable who was being bullied - it would have been abnormal if she had suspected anything else. Yet Mrs Bent continued to do one extraordinary thing after another. She dismissed Elizabeth's story as delusional, opened up a file on her and appointed herself as Elizabeth's social worker, the one to take care of her mental health.

Meanwhile Mrs Elders and Elizabeth didn't even know what an ASW was. They didn't know that some social workers specialise in psychiatry; they thought they were all the same.

As Mrs Bent worked a lot with the elderly, and because she was asking questions about Paul Stalker's harassment, they both assumed it was Mrs Elders she had come to help. But in fact it was Paul Stalker she was acting for; and she had a secret agenda of her own. When Mrs Bent saw the big house Elizabeth stood to inherit, she was viciously jealous. She thought it was a dreadful injustice that such a woman should have such a property, and did not like the close relationship Elizabeth shared with her mother. She seemed determined to break it all up, from sheer resentment.

She wanted to be able to say that Elizabeth was paranoid and mentally ill. From the moment she first saw her, she wanted to have her sectioned. She telephoned her own doctor and asked him to do it, but he refused. She told her director that she had no grounds for having her sectioned, as Elizabeth was accepting medication from her own doctor. But this was nonsense. Elizabeth was on no medication whatsoever, and had proved time and again that she didn't need it. It was the beginning of Mrs Bent getting everything wrong. She could not even get him to refer her to a psychiatrist.

Mrs Bent was also made to feel inadequate by the tireless charity work the two women did. She wanted to put a stop to it all, to gain control. She had no right to claim that everything Elizabeth was telling her was delusional; only a doctor can make such a diagnosis. Yet neither Mrs Elders nor her daughter had any idea about what she was up to, and for some time they went on letting her inside the house. They never imagined for a second that she was coming to see Elizabeth as a patient. Nor did they imagine just how much trouble was ahead.

Mrs Bent would be certain to put up the defence that she was simply trying to help. This way she would be covered by the Mental Health Act 1983. However she would have had to produce a report to support such a claim and when it emerged that no such assistance was required then a court would never accept it. It is very sad that in cases like this, so often, patients discover their rights too late. It can in any case, frequently be too difficult to get one's own side of the story properly listened to, and it can also be very expensive.

Mrs Bent also diagnosed Mrs Elders as having dementia. Again, she had no right to do this; it has to be done by a qualified psychiatrist. Yet she was stating this as a fact. The diagnosis was later challenged by both Mrs Elders' solicitor and her doctor.

These diagnoses from an unqualified social worker were extraordinary, not only because neither Elizabeth nor her mother were not in any way disturbed but because their stories were so typical of someone vulnerable being picked upon, especially if there is money involved.

* * * * * * * * * *

Mrs Bent got in early that night. She was glad she lived on her own. She wanted to go her own way and have no one on her back.

She had been thinking deeply about Elizabeth and her mother, and that night she had a dream. She dreamed she could see the future, and in it she saw Mrs Elders dying. A doctor was standing with Elizabeth by her bedside and the doctor was telling Elizabeth she had managed admirably. When she awoke, this dream greatly troubled her. It could so easily come true. It wasn't only that Elizabeth was managing so well - she had worked as a nurse on geriatric units. How easy it must be to have just one patient to care for, especially someone you love so much.

Mrs Bent couldn't bear to think of it. She wasn't at all sure if she was fit to be with old people. How dreadful if someone like Elizabeth proved to be better. This was when she began her determined campaign to get Elizabeth put into a mental hospital. She wanted her put away, right out of the way, and then the worry of it all would be gone. She would then feel confident that she was the one who was stable and sensible, the one who should be in charge, and she would be able to get control over the lives of both Elizabeth and her mother. She would then feel adequate again.

Later the director wrote in a letter: 'Elizabeth refuses to accept that Mrs Bent was merely carrying out her duties under the Mental Health Act.' No court would have accepted it either.

Meanwhile Paul Stalker was getting deep into his scheming. Every morning he would start by driving over to the Elders' home. He had plenty of time because he had money and did not need to work. He pretended he wanted to help, and as he had a social worker to support him he was covered by the Mental Health Act. It is said about men like him, 'The dominator is his name, controlling women is his game', and so it was. He wanted to break them both, to make them both weak, so that he could be in complete charge. He also very much enjoyed upsetting them both – they were women, so he hated them.

Mrs Bent and her colleagues were willing to believe practically anything Paul Stalker said, yet clearly he was talking malicious nonsense - he had a history of it. He was a known hater of women. In the past he had been called 'the entertainer' or 'the comedian' and his complaining was sometimes referred to as 'The Paul Stalker Show'. He was doing and saying things which people found hilarious, but Mrs Bent refused to look into any of it. Instead she accepted everything he said.

He would put his face to the window, laugh his mad laugh, flash his mad look and tell Elizabeth he had murdered a woman. He wanted her to look mad when she repeated it. He would follow her in his car, stop by her side, let her walk on for a bit and then drive up and do it again.

He would hang about the woods just opposite the house, or the churchyard they passed every day. He managed time and again to get the key to their house to let himself in, and while he was there he would help himself to her post, her address book or her diary. He would steam the letters open, read them, seal them back up again and then put them back into the letterbox. No one would know it was the second time they'd arrived there.

He also photocopied her address book. He knew when she'd be out, and when he could take it and put it back without her knowing. He would then make suggestive remarks about some of the things he'd seen inside.

He would send nasty letters to Mrs Elders inviting her to afternoon tea. He would wind her up and get her going with pretty little invitations, though she would always tell him she didn't want to go. He would say, 'Come on, lovely chicken
sandwiches, lovely and juicy!' knowing full well she was practically a vegan, she hated the killing of animals so much.

She sent one of his letters back. She had written on it 'This is such a masterpiece of being nasty that I thought you might like it back so that you can use it again.' Someone else added 'so that he can frame it.'

For Christmas, again because he knew she hated the killing of animals, he sent her a pair of leather gloves with rabbit fur lining. Next to the label that said 'rabbit fur' he had pinned on a note saying 'with love.'

He brought in his own phone and plugged it into the wall. He said it would be all right as it was his employer's phone and any calls he made on it would register on his employer's bill and he would pay it. Mrs Elders was very surprised. She didn't think he had ever heard of work. She did know he never did any, as he was round at her house the whole of the time making a nuisance of himself.

* * * * * * * * *

Elizabeth had an older sister called Sisley. When Sisley found out how much support Social Services were giving to Paul Stalker while giving none to Elizabeth or her mother, she joined in – to help Stalker. She gave him all the support she could. She too wanted control over Elizabeth's life and her mother's.

I would call it a typical example of what Women's Aid would call a headworker, as it's so similar to those cases where men hate women and try to control them. Sisley was trying to manipulate Elizabeth's mind the whole time, telling her she was stupid, and up to a point she was succeeding. Elizabeth accepted it. I think the trouble is that we are brought up to believe that we have to accept criticism, to accept we can't always be right, and we finish up by accepting it all when we shouldn't be accepting any of it. It can do enormous damage, damage which takes a great deal of undoing.

Sisley didn't need any more money. She lived in a big house and had a very big garden, but although Mrs Elders had always been the perfect mother, Sisley had never done a thing to help. She would only turn up if there was money about, and she always wanted more of it. Her husband Ronald had attacked Elizabeth while she had looked on and done nothing. It is far commoner for people with a history of mental health problems to be attacked by others than for them to do the attacking.

In Elizabeth's case, when she complained about it, they denied it and used it as evidence that she was mentally ill. Of course Mrs Bent gave them both her full support.

Sisley was the sister who had always had everything, who had had good luck all her life. She was born clever and had done well at school, while Elizabeth had struggled. Having despised her little sister from the start, Sisley had to show her how much better she was – and she never grew out of it. She was always telling Elizabeth she wasn't clever, that it was she who went to the best school and wore the best uniform. She would bring her friends in from school and tell jokes about Elizabeth in front of them, making her feel small and ridiculous.

When Elizabeth became a teenager and started wearing high heeled shoes and nylon stockings, Sisley would sneer at her and tell her she looked absurd and that she wasn't old enough to dress like that. She said she only looked nice in her school shoes and socks. She would also tell her she wasn't old enough to go out with boys. She enjoyed making her look small and silly.

Sisley had always had good health, while Elizabeth had been prone to illness. Sisley was much better looking and it was always she who got all of the boys. Now she was married to a man with money and had made some of her own, and Elizabeth was poor compared with her. Sisley had a grown-up family, while Elizabeth only had her mother and would have no one after she was dead. Sisley had put so much poison into the minds of her grown-up children about Elizabeth that she had wrecked any sort of a relationship she might one day be able to have with them. She wanted to have more and more of everything. She wanted all the money and all the power.

That night Mrs Bent had another dream, one which troubled her for days. She dreamed that when she took her clothes off at night, there was a man up a tree just outside her bedroom window who was peeping in on her, spying on her between the curtains, watching her. Yet there was no tree outside her bedroom window. Was she going mad?

She began to think about Elizabeth. There was a tree outside Elizabeth's bedroom window. As she pondered the dream the next day, she decided to put the blame on to Elizabeth. She wrote in her report, 'Elizabeth says Paul Stalker is up an oak tree spying on her.' (She got that wrong – it was a beech tree, Elizabeth would never have called it an oak.)

The next night she dreamed again. She saw an elderly lady, small and slim with grey hair tied back in a bun. Gently, in a comforting voice, the woman asked her, 'What did you say that for? Elizabeth has never said that about a man in a tree'. Mrs Bent wanted to contradict her, to say she had, but something told her not to, as she felt afraid. She was very mixed up. Practically shouting it aloud, she told herself again and again, 'Elizabeth DID tell me that, she DID say a man was spying on her from up an oak tree!' Then quietly, remembering the smoothing voice of the elderly lady, she laid her head back on to the pillow and drifted off to sleep.

It was nearly four in the morning when Mrs Bent woke again. It was May and soon it would be light, so she decided to get up and go out for a drive. She went to Elizabeth's house and parked the car at the top of the road, on a hill. It was getting light and the birds were singing. As she walked down to the house she saw pink blossom on the trees. Blossom was everywhere; it was beautiful. She turned into Elizabeth's garden. She loved the garden, the house, the village, everything about it.

She looked up at the window where she knew Elizabeth would be sleeping and the beech tree just outside her bedroom window. She sat on the ground beside it, leaned against it, and wished she'd had brought her picnic basket with her. She began to daydream. She gazed at the house. 'Maybe one day all that will be mine' she thought.

* * * * * * * * * *

Up until now Paul Stalker had only vaguely suggested to Mrs Bent that he had been slandered by Elizabeth. She began to wonder what would happen if he took her to court. Would it mean he would get the house, and if he did would he let her have some of the money? Perhaps he would give her a lot of money; after all she had given him assurances that she would give him great support. She also knew she should keep sweet with Elizabeth's sister. But thoughts like this, about money, didn't often race away with her. They stayed mainly at the back of her mind. Her main interest, her real drive, was to get control.

Soon she knew it was time to go, and she reluctantly got up and began to stroll away. Elizabeth rolled over in bed. Something had woken her. A dog started barking. She leaned across the window and peeped out between the bedroom curtains. Had someone just walked through the garden gate? She couldn't be sure.

The next day one of the Elders' lodgers said he had seen a woman in the garden. Maybe it was someone visiting next door. Neither of them thought about it again until some time later.

When Mrs Bent arrived at work next day, Paul Stalker was waiting for her. She recognised him at once; she'd already seen a photograph of him and it was one she would remember as it reminded her so much of her father. She also recognised his voice, as they had spoken a lot on the phone. Again he expressed his 'concern' for Mrs Elders and her care. He was anxious to remain well covered by the Mental Health Act.

Stalker reminded Mrs Bent of her father, not only because of his looks but because of his manner. It was something she had always found impossible to face up to, that she'd had a terrible father. She still hankered after love, love to give to the man her father had never been, so she listened intensely to Paul Stalker, anxious to please him. She was completely blind to what he really was like, and refused to accept any of the evidence other people had tried to give her. Her drive to support him was very strong, and nothing could move it.

She had been like that with other men; when she fell for a man she would do anything for him. As a young student at college, she had been notorious for it. Other girls had tried to tell her, 'You don't have to do what he says', but she would not listen.

At times Mrs Bent would become highly indignant about it. 'How dare they tell me what to do!' she would shout. She felt it should be her telling other people what to do. She found she hadn't got the same charisma she'd had at school, but she did hope she'd get some of it back again.

She remembered those days, and how very satisfying they had been. She would lead the other girls on in the playground, get a crowd up together and pick on one person. They would chase the victim all round the place, point a finger at her, laugh and jeer at her and make her cry. Then they would call her a cry baby. It didn't matter what they said as long as it was something insulting. 'You smell!' was one of her favourites, and another was 'You live in a titchy little house in the slums!'

Sisley, knowing that she had a social worker well and truly on her side, began to get drunk with success. She wrote in a letter about her husband, 'Ronald is very stern, he stands no nonsense.' Mrs Elders wrote back and said, 'Who does he think he is? The headmaster of Eton? I suggest he sees a psychiatrist, it sounds like delusions of grandeur. It could get serious.'

It was very serious for Elizabeth that Mrs Bent had taken Sisley's side, accepting that Ronald hadn't been violent and that the only help Elizabeth needed was social and psychiatric. It could be giving them a lot of power, or at least influence. But far worse than that, after Mrs Elders was dead, she would be the nearest relative. This might well mean she'd get some power over her little sister. It was very, very dangerous.

At least they had a good neighbour, Mrs Simpson. She had been more than willing to help when Mrs Elders had been ill, and with other things too. So had her mother when she was there. Such things can be so important; in fact they can be everything. They might make all the difference as to whether someone old has to go into a home.

Yet it was only Mrs Elders' rightful reward. When she had been young herself there had been an old man living next door with a mother who lived to be 102 years old. They were Russians who had escaped the revolution, and the mother had once been a princess. Mrs Elders had been more than happy to help them at any time. But now Sisley was wrecking everything. Mrs Simpson was beginning to wonder what she was getting involved in.

Now Sisley did something really devious; she used the power of tears. She knocked on Mrs Simpson's door and pretended to cry. She told her how worried she was about her old mother, and for a week or two Mrs Simpson was completely taken in. Sisley left her phone number: 'I wish Elizabeth could have help. I'm so worried about her!' she said. 'You will call me, won't you, if there is a crisis?'

The neighbour agreed. It never crossed her mind that it was all a scheme to get money out of Mrs Elders. But then Sisley did something even worse than that; she told Mrs Simpson about Elizabeth's psychiatric history. It was almost blackmail. Yet Sisley took a delight in writing to Elizabeth and telling her she'd done it. She knew full well how much Elizabeth feared the sort of 'help' she was talking about and how crucial it was that no one knew about her history. It was a case of, 'If you don't do as you are told, this is what you'll get.'

Then Sisley came out with something horrendous. She said that Elizabeth was one of these neurotic women who dream it up that a man had assaulted her. This is something that would frighten a lot of people, and especially men. Yet Elizabeth had also met women who would steer clear of other women who had such dreams. Elizabeth would do the same herself. She would condemn another woman if she thought she was accusing an innocent man. Elizabeth feared she would have no friends left if her sister was going to spread it around that she'd done this.

Sisley said, 'All my husband did was shout at her. She took it so seriously that she started saying he'd been physically violent.'

But Mrs Simpson soon started ignoring what Sisley was telling her. She immediately respected Mrs Elders' wishes. When Mrs Elders told her, 'In no circumstances are you to contact my other daughter', Mrs Simpson told her, 'I won't - in fact I can't. I've destroyed her number.'

To others Sisley was calling Elizabeth a thief and accusing her of taking her mother's post. Some people might suspect this meant she herself was taking it, and that it was another case of transference of guilt. They might especially wonder that after Paul Stalker had been caught red-handed taking it. It can be dreadful to be a victim of someone's guilty conscience; you can be made ill with it. Maybe he had just been giving her parts to read. They would be able to justify it together by saying that their interest was to help.

Elizabeth did have a little house of her own, which she loved. Yet she had to spend more and more time at her mother's, because Stalker was making such a nuisance of himself. Eventually she had to move in there altogether. She and her mother had hired a private detective some time ago, but now they stepped it up even more and got more records of what was happening. This is a grey area as regards the law. It's not so much what you get on camera or tape as what you do with it after. Anything they had was always kept by the detective.

'Don't think I'm happy with this arrangement, I would dearly love to be able to live in my own home again' Elizabeth wrote in a letter to her sister, but Sisley didn't answer. She did however use it later as an excuse to leave everything for Elizabeth to do. Her excuse was that their mother was 'putting a roof over her head.'

The Elders' home had six floors including the cellars, and was sometimes called the 'house of stairs', because there were so many. The rooms in which Elizabeth had once played with other children, where she and her friends had had parties as teenagers, had long lain empty. This also made them quite spooky, and Mrs Elders became more and more afraid to go upstairs. Not without reason. They would sometimes go and find Paul Stalker there, hiding.

Elizabeth didn't know which was worse, the nightmares or the insomnia. One dream she kept having was that she was trapped in the attic and could hear her sister and brother-in-law coming up the stairs. The dream came back even if she slept downstairs on the couch in her own home. How wonderful it would be to see the light coming in through the curtains, hear the sound of milk bottles clicking, hear a train go thundering past and know it was next morning. Then she would go for a walk in the park, smell the flowers and enjoy what she could while she could, for she feared so much that it would all shortly be coming to an end.

One night as she lay dozing she remembered an incident that had happened some time before. It had been most dramatic, but not realising how very evil Paul Stalker was she had decided it was something she should forget. It had happened when she had stayed out late one night. There had been only Stalker and her mother in the house, and in the middle of that night he had woken her mother up and said, 'Quick! Quick! Fetch the police, there are burglars in the attic!' Then, very convincingly, he rushed up the stairs as if to challenge them

'Paul! Are you sure?' called Mrs Elders.

'Yes! Dial 999!' he called down. He made her feel it would be irresponsible, even dangerous, not to call the police, so she did as he said. When they arrived he went to the front door and denied he had ever said there were burglars. 'I AM sorry to have wasted your time, she's ALWAYS doing things like that,' he said.

Elizabeth arrived in the house in the middle of it all. Not knowing then how evil he was, but knowing what a fool he could be, she had merely thought he felt embarrassed, maybe even that he'd get into some trouble for causing a false alarm. She was certain he really did believe that he had heard something. Elizabeth could tell that the police weren't all that put out by it; they were used to this sort of thing, and their interest was really to get on to their next call. It was something they'd soon forget, so she wasn't going to do anything to draw attention to it.

But now she knew he was thoroughly evil. Now she realised that he had intended using the ruse as evidence that her mother was deranged, and later she was to discover that this was a typical trick for a man who wants control. She would never have dreamed at that time that he would one day get the support of Social Services, or that there is nothing in the Mental Health Act to say that opinions have got to be based on facts, and that even if there had been witnesses to say they had heard him tell Mrs Elders to do this a mental health team could still refuse to check up. They could still act entirely upon what he had said and treat Mrs Elders as a dippy old woman.

Elizabeth had also once suspected that Stalker was moving and hiding things in order to make it look as though her mother was going senile, especially when he would say she needed to go on tranquillizers. She didn't dare say so, because that would go down as paranoia.

Elizabeth realised she had slipped up very badly when admitting that she had a psychiatric history. What a can of worms it had opened.

*Oh what a tangled web we weave when first we decide
to never deceive*

*Oh what a mess we can find ourselves in, a story so
long where do we begin?*

*We cannot be firm, we cannot be polite, if the interest
of someone is only to fight*

*If it's only control they want on their side, then we must
tell lies in order to hide.*

Alice Frank 2012

Chapter Two

THE MIND OF PAUL STALKER

Meanwhile Paul Stalker continued to shock people with his evil ways. He'd do things people had never thought or heard of before. For one thing he believed a woman did not have the right to refuse him or leave him, and he would seek revenge if she did. No one could understand why he wanted a woman in the first place. He would be so unpleasant once he'd snared her, and then there'd be a big commotion when she left him. One woman, a teacher at an infants' school, had to take the morning off work because he had upset her so much the night before. He had caused so much trouble at her house that she'd had to call the police. There was no point in telling her he was making someone ill. He didn't care.

One girl who fell victim to him was German. After they had a row he started persistently telephoning her, sometimes in the middle of the night, and talking about the war. 'We've had two wars with Germany and we won them both you know' he once said. 'It's three actually' she replied.

Yet it was his mother he seemed to hate the most. He would get quite vicious if ever the subject of her came up. This frightened women very much. Remember that man in the Hitchcock film

Psycho - all that behaviour was supposed to be on account of his mother. A lot of it frightened women very much. They also found it sinister.

He found these girls' fathers a terrible nuisance. They would be hanging about the whole time keeping an eye on him. They were afraid he would do something terrible to their daughters. It upset Mrs Elders very much when she realised that it was seriously considered that her own nephew might kill someone, but knowing him she could quite believe it.

Stalker joined a drama group, but soon left because they didn't give him a part in a play. That was very typical of him. Everyone was glad to see him go. 'What a nasty man' they all said. Then the cleaners received a bouquet of flowers from him. It made them begin to wonder if he was a nice man after all - until they got the bill for them the next day.

We all remember the day when the word 'spastic' started being misused. People started using it as a term of ridicule, and the condition it referred to was thereafter known as cerebral palsy. Paul Stalker was one of those who liked using it as a term of abuse.

One day Stalker was round at Mrs Elders' when the sound cut out on the television. It was only for a minute, but he went away to make a phone call to the broadcasting company to complain. When Mrs Elders realised this she was not at all happy because she didn't want her phone using for this. The next day there was a story in the papers about the number of people who had phoned up the broadcaster just because the sound had cut out for a moment. It talked as though they were cranks.

Stalker suffered greatly from road rage. He thought everybody should get out of his way, would hoot at the slightest thing and couldn't bring himself to wait for a second. It was a wonder he'd never been punched on the nose. When he was doing it it took a bit of time for people to realise that one car was making all the noise. The only time Elizabeth had ever heard anything like it before was once when she had seen a lorry spilling potatoes all over the road. Lots of people were blowing their horns to try to tell him. And so it was when Paul Stalker was going along the road - people were looking all around them, expecting to see something like potatoes all over the place.

One day a middle-aged woman was trying to cross the road carrying heavy shopping bags. She had seen her bus on the other side of the road was anxious not to miss it. Stalker was driving along with Mrs Elders in the car. He started cursing when he saw the woman and wasn't going to let her cross. Mrs Elders started shrieking at him, 'Don't you dare make her miss her bus!' No one had ever heard her play hell like that before.

He believed there was nothing more important than speed. You judged a man's driving by how fast he could go. Yet at the same time he didn't mind holding everyone else up. He was very good at blocking people in. He was also very slow at moving his car when asked to. It was a wonder no one ever let his tyres down.

Mrs Elders was very annoyed when she found out one day that he had been next door to complain about the neighbours' workmen. The neighbours and the workmen wanted to know who he was. One of the workmen assumed it was the noise he was complaining about, but it was the dust; he was saying that the dust was going to do serious damage to his health. This assumption did not matter, but it mattered a great deal when Mrs Bent was making assumptions and acting on them, as will become clear later.

The time when he complained about the neighbours' workmen, Mrs Elders went rushing across to apologise because she feared it might cause bad relations with them. One of the workmen seemed to be about 14, although he must have been at least 16 as he had left school. Mrs. Elders said afterwards about him, "He wasn't laughing or even smiling, yet I could tell he thought it was funny, I suppose they get some tuition in this sort of thing."

She found out later how very right she was. The firm which employed him sent him to college for half a day a week. Her lodgers, all university students, then started making jokes about it and saying, "If you have any work to do with him around the place you have to go to college first to learn how to keep your face straight."

When Mrs Elders was talking with friends about Paul Stalker one day, one of them said 'It's dreadful, all this criticism. We've got to try to think of something he does right, something we can praise him about.' They all sat and thought. Then Mrs Elders said, 'This is terrible. We all come from a family of school teachers, professionals at giving people confidence, but none of us can think of anything good to say about him.'

Some people put up with Stalker's actions just because they didn't want to upset his aunt. One day when she had workmen in the house, she heard one of them say about him, 'If he said that to me he'd be straight down them stairs and he'd land on his backside.' She didn't want to know what it was about.

Unfortunately his nasty streak ran in the family. He had a great aunt who was always complaining. She had sent her son to a very good public school, and people were always hearing about what ructions she had been causing in the headmaster's office, though in a school like that most people hardly ever saw the head. When the other mothers heard about it, they said, 'How does she get inside there? I can never get to see him!' And so it was with him. When people heard about his complaints, say for example in the supermarket, or in the manager's office, they would wonder how he had got in. It caused very serious problems for vulnerable people if Social Services took his complaints seriously, yet refused to investigate the facts behind them.

Paul Stalker never understood that his behaviour wasn't normal, and that not everyone lived as he did. One night when he went into a pub he met some youths who took him on to a night club. He behaved so badly that the next day two of the youths had to go back to the club to apologise for taking him there. He thought it was an everyday occurrence, people having to apologise on your behalf for your unpleasant behaviour.

It also annoyed Mrs Elders very much that he thought he had some authority inside her house. He would tell her lodgers to tidy their things out of the hall. Mrs Elders would shout at him to keep out of it and make it clear to everyone else that he had no right to do this.

Another time when some students were play-fighting on the stairs, she called up to them, 'You break those banisters and there WILL be trouble!' Then Paul started joining in, telling them off. She was furious. She didn't want the students to hear how angry she was so she hissed quietly into his ear 'Will you leave it to me!' But they heard just the same. Later Elizabeth heard them making jokes about it. They were saying, 'Thou shalt not break the banisters.'

One day Elizabeth came in to hear the tail end of a conversation going on upstairs between Paul and a lodger. The lodger was saying to him, 'You keep your nose out of it or you'll get it squashed.' He wouldn't mind his own business.

One day after a row with Elizabeth and Mrs Elders, Stalker phoned the Inland Revenue and told them Mrs Elders was fiddling her taxes. A man came round to the house about it and spoke to Mrs Elders. He explained it all to her and finished up by saying that he would accept what she had told them and would not take any notice of what others said. They meant they were discounting what Stalker had told them. Mrs Elders already knew that her tax affairs were between her and the Inland Revenue and no one else, but she later discovered that she had to share them with one department only.

When Stalker started hanging about the churchyard across the road from the public house, it began to become unnerving. Elizabeth tried to get witnesses, but of course people do not remember casual strangers who pass in the street. Elizabeth was uncomfortable about having to explain to people why it was important to remember if they had seen him. She would explain that she had a psychiatric history, which meant her word wasn't credible - she could be hallucinating. Indeed, by now Social Services had brainwashed her into believing there really was something the matter with her.

That night Mrs Bent had another dream. It started off as a nightmare with planes flying about. Then suddenly, as if she had woken up, the aircraft noise turned into a sweet melody and she was walking around a lovely garden. Then she found herself in a churchyard. It was night time, pitch black, and she had gone to meet Paul Stalker, who was waiting for her in his car. It gave her a tremendous feeling of peace.

Finally she awoke. 'Lucky no one knew I had that dream' she thought as she drifted back to sleep. Next morning she wrote in her report, 'Elizabeth says Paul Stalker is frequently in his car in the churchyard at night.' Elizabeth had never said that he was in his car, and she had said it had happened during the day, yet Mrs Bent had talked as though she had said it happened at night. 'Are you afraid to go out at night with him about?' she had asked her.

Now that it was spring, people from the pub opposite the churchyard started drinking outside. Elizabeth managed to get two of them to confirm that they had seen Paul Stalker, but Mrs Bent refused to speak to them. It began to get more spooky as Mrs Bent continued to insist that it was all delusional, including the statement that he was in America at the precise time Elizabeth and Mrs Elders said they had seen him in the churchyard. Mrs Edlers commented, 'It's eerie that is, it's spooky to say that.'

Then Elizabeth did a bit of checking up, and found out he had just been on holiday to New York. Clearly he had rushed from the airport to be there at the time he knew Elizabeth walked past every day. He had hoped that the people in America wouldn't remember exactly what time they last saw him, and would be willing to give him an alibi.

Then another social worker phoned him, leading him to believe that she had seen him there herself, so he had to admit to it. He said he had been waiting for someone. Both Mrs Elders and Elizabeth were on cloud nine with such reliable evidence, and in any case they hadn't much wanted to ask the people outside the pub. But hope turned to despair when yet again Mrs Bent refused to check up. She refused to consult the other social worker, even though they worked together in the same office.

Mrs Bent continued to be adamant that Stalker hadn't been in the churchyard. She continued to write in her reports that the sightings were delusional, and to get what Elizabeth had said wrong.

One day Elizabeth came in and found her mother crying. While she had been watching television, Paul Stalker had put his face to the window and refused to go away. He had laughed his mad laugh and then gone on staring at her, only pausing to flash the crazy look in his eye. She had shouted 'Go away! Go away!'

Elizabeth and a neighbour found footprints in the flower bed exactly where she said she had seen him. After this they moved the TV upstairs so they could watch it without his interference. When Mrs Bent came round the next day she refused either to look at the footprints or to ask the neighbours, who had also seen them, but she was willing to look at where they'd moved the television to. She then called it 'acting upon delusions'. She was happy to check on anything that might add to her 'evidence' that the Elders were deluded.

The Elders now began to live permanently upstairs, even taking the cooking stove with them. That would demonstrate to most people how deeply Stalker's actions were affecting them, but to Mrs Bent it was all part of 'having fixed delusions'. They were afraid to go into the hall in case he was standing on the front doorstep looking in on them. They were even afraid to go out into the garden, as they'd found him hanging about the gate so much. When they did leave the house they would climb over a bank into someone else's garden to get out to the road. He had a social worker on his side, so all he had to do was to complain to her. She supported him in everything.

When they moved the television upstairs the first programme they saw on it was about some monks who had lived peacefully on an island until bandits arrived and took over the place. They wrecked everything, and the lives of the monks were never the same again. Elizabeth and her mother felt like the monks. Like them, they had been used to a quiet life and had been completely unprepared.

Some people seemed to imagine that Elizabeth was so desperate that she might try to kill Stalker. She noticed that when they spoke to her about it, their only concern in it was for her. 'I don't want you to go to prison' they would say. She realised then that people knew how bad he was. No one had any feeling for him.

One day Elizabeth telephoned Stalker's local police about the harassment. 'No, it's the police in Grimley, where you live, who should be seeing to this' she was very sharply told. Yet for some reason the Grimley police hadn't thought it was their problem. He was known to the police, and so notorious that they were falling out about which station should be dealing with him.

It infuriated Elizabeth when Mrs Bent talked to Elizabeth about Paul Stalker's 'rights'. Elizabeth would almost scream at her, 'What about ME? What about MY rights?' And Mrs Bent would offer her psychiatric treatment and talk about how she would have to live with her condition, just as people have to live with diabetes or arthritis. She insisted on regarding Elizabeth as having a mental problem.

At the time, even Elizabeth did not realise to what extent Mrs Bent was dismissing everything as delusional. Nor did she know that Mrs Bent had false beliefs, and such beliefs can be very fixed. She would never accept that Stalker was harassing them. So Elizabeth, would scream at her, 'No I won't have psychiatric treatment! If you think it's driving me mad, then take away the cause. He has to be stopped!'

Then Elizabeth and her mother had an idea – to ask Stalker's neighbours if they could give their support. They wrote to them all, and two of them called at their home to see them about it. They knew enough about him to tell the police, enough for the police to be able to take action. The police then assured both Elizabeth and Mrs Elders 'You'll have no more trouble from him. We have dealt with him.'

They were both delighted at the prospect of being liberated from their curse at last. Elizabeth was in a state of euphoria. 'Unbelievable!' She said. 'I am free to go back and live in my own home, free to have a phone, free to go out of the front gate!' The list of what they were now free to do went on and on.

But Elizabeth was right to call it unbelievable. It wasn't true. Social Services wrecked the lot of it. After Paul Stalker came out of the police station, he went crying to them about it. He said that what she had written about him was libel, and that he hadn't been harassing them. He put in a request for her to have her mental health assessed and they granted it to him and gave him their full support. They were most sympathetic.

Mrs Bent told Elizabeth that she was no longer free to refuse psychiatric treatment. She had to remain at home, and then she might have to go into hospital. They had started the procedure to have her committed.

* * * * * * * * * *

That night Mrs Bent had another dream. She dreamed that she was writing her report and there was someone outside in the dark looking in on her, yet whenever she turned round to look there was no one there. She would merely catch a glimpse of someone dash very quickly away from the window. She knew it was an elderly, slim woman, though not the one she'd seen in the other dream.

She got on with writing the report, but decided not to sign it. She felt afraid; no one must know who wrote it. She put it in the post instead and when it turned up next day she told everyone it was from an anonymous source. That was accepted.

The next day it didn't worry her that much as she knew she hadn't really done what was in the dream, but she did go round to see Elizabeth. She said to her, 'Now you signed the letters you wrote; you weren't anonymous.' As though that was at least one good thing Elizabeth had done. It was insulting to suggest she might do such a thing, but Elizabeth was beginning to accept it as the norm. A social worker could throw insult after insult at you.

Yet it still puzzled Elizabeth. What point would there be in writing a letter and not signing it? If no one knows who you are they can't help you. Elizabeth didn't know at that point that Mrs Bent was dismissing everything she was saying as delusional, and was also claiming that Elizabeth was being nothing short of malicious.

'It's a very strange thing for her to say' commented Mrs Elders. 'Yet I can understand how she might want to be anonymous herself, with all that she's saying about you - and what's all this about an eye having to be kept on you? That's yet another thing that's back to front. It's not you that needs watching, it's her when she's writing reports.'

Elizabeth and Mrs Elders had obtained legal advice, but later they wished they had sought a psychologist's opinion as well, because it would have helped them to predict some of what the social workers, and in particular Mrs Bent, would do next. During the Second World

War psychologists predicted that Hitler would spend less and less time in the public eye, which is just what he did. He would hide away in his home on the mountains. Afterwards the psychologists said how unfortunate it was that the Government had not asked their opinion before Chamberlain went to Germany to agree a peace treaty. They would have been able to tell him Hitler would not keep it.

Although Paul Stalker was a notorious liar and a well-known whiner, Social Services continued to take everything he said seriously and refused to investigate any of Elizabeth's complaints about him. They also continued to make serious mistakes. They claimed she had been writing letters to his employers, even though he never did any work. He told them it could interfere with some promotion he had just put in for, and they believed him and acted upon it.

Stalker had not only put in a request for Elizabeth to have her mental health assessed, he had also asked for her to be sectioned, although under the Mental Health Act only a nearest relative can do either of these things. Mrs Elders protested in the strongest terms and put in a request that they should get legal advice, confirm that Paul Stalker's allegations about libel were not correct and that it had nothing to do with mental health or with them. But they wouldn't do it, even though she was still considered by her doctor and solicitor to be of sound mind. They did what Paul Stalker wanted.

Mrs Elders and Elizabeth went to see the Social Services Team Leader about it, but again it was a waste of time. She was on Mrs Bent's side. She did agree that Mrs Bent should not investigate Stalker's complaints, although she was acting on them. She reassured them, saying Elizabeth could appeal 10 to 21 days after they had had her committed, and a tribunal would then investigate it.

Later when they were asked why they had not looked at the letters they alleged Elizabeth had written, which Mrs Bent was using as evidence to get her sectioned, they said that to look at them would be a breach of confidentiality. Mrs Bent hadn't seen them – she had guessed what they'd said. Either that or she had taken Paul Stalker's word for it. Social Services also said that their interest in it was for Elizabeth. They were well covered by the Mental Health Act, which says you can do all kinds of things if you are claiming they are to help the patient, but does not say opinions have to be based on fact. This was the first of a series of terrible shocks for Elizabeth and her mother about what can be done in the name of care.

You can make someone mad simply by saying they're mad, especially if it's someone vulnerable. But you can also do it by putting them on drugs, which has been common in China and communist Russia.

Chapter Three

MRS BENT'S OBSESSION

Although it was only hearsay, Elizabeth was very frightened when she heard what power the ministers were talking of giving mental health teams if the patient was unable to understand that it was in their interests to help them. She feared there would be nothing to follow to say opinions have to be based on fact. This is mentioned in the Code of Practice, but that is not nearly so powerful.

It can be just as dangerous if they are saying you are a threat to yourself as it is if they are saying you're a threat to someone else. Elizabeth told them that if she had to have a social worker, she didn't want it to be Mrs Bent. By now she had been brainwashed into believing she needed one. They told her she had to have Mrs Bent.

Mrs Elders told the team leader she wouldn't allow them to put her daughter in a mental hospital. They later found out that the Social Services team intended to bring the police with them when they came for her. Yet all the team leader said at the time was that the only way they could guarantee there wouldn't be a scene out in the street was if Elizabeth agreed to get quietly get into the ambulance. She said she doubted very much that she would be allowed out into the hospital grounds or to leave the ward, and most certainly she would not be allowed to go home. She said the police would be called if she did and they would bring her back straight away. She said she didn't know how often she would be able to see her mother. It was up to the hospital to decide when she would be able to have visitors.

That night Mrs Bent decided to have an early night. She made herself a cup of coffee after her bath and sat quietly in her nightclothes in the back room downstairs.

Suddenly she heard a bang. It made her jump. Was it the old man across the way who had been cantankerous before? She could soon sort him out. Then, for a moment, she thought someone was in her garden.

She would sometimes keep her curtains drawn, because she didn't want anyone looking in and seeing how untidy it all was. If they came round the back and looked through the window, they might see a pile of stationery on the table or something else she had brought home from work. At times she found such material very handy; twice she had managed to intimidate someone vulnerable by writing a letter to them on headed notepaper. They hadn't realised it was only a personal matter and didn't know it was only from a neighbour. They hadn't put a name to a face, and in any case they didn't know she was a social worker She had also disguised her signature.

She quietly and quickly got up to open a drawer and hide it all away, but as she did so there was another bang. This time she went to the window to look out, but she couldn't see anything. She decided she'd had enough and it was time to go to bed.

She was soon asleep, and she began to dream. It was another nightmare. She was back at work, writing up the notes, and a voice shouted at her loud and clear, 'You are not to use headed notepaper from Social Services to say that!'

She looked all around to see who it was, but no one was there.

She was very frightened, for she wondered what else they knew about her. It seemed to be a man, someone rough, someone big. Who was this invisible person? How long had he been watching her? Did he know she had been taking these papers home with her for some time, and had they seen her when, exhausted with it all, she had chucked it in the bin? It had put the wind up her when she'd read in the papers of a postman who had been caught letting the post pile up in his own home or chucking it in the river instead of delivering it.

Some time later she discovered that she had thrown away some quite important documents. She just had to keep her fingers crossed and hope it would never be noticed.

She continued to look around the room, getting desperate, but still she could not see anyone. 'I've got to use it, I'm a social worker!' she howled. And then a voice, soft and gentle said, 'In that case you have to.'

She awoke at that and lay quietly in her bed for a while. When she drifted off to sleep again, the voice came back. It explained it all to her. It confirmed her suspicions that Elizabeth had been pilfering from a charity; this was a great relief to her, for she had been wanting to believe this for some time.

She went to work next morning very happy. The first thing she did was get out Elizabeth's notes to write up about it. She gave the name of the charity Elizabeth had taken headed notepaper from and added that Elizabeth had written 'libel' on it. She now felt enormously relieved and felt she had nothing to feel guilty about. She had offloaded the lot of it. She now felt free to use any paper she liked and to write whatever she liked on it. It wouldn't be pilfering and it wouldn't be libel, it could only be that if Elizabeth did it.

But she didn't stay calm for long. She started to get upset again as she scribbled away, and by the time she had it ready for the clerk to type out she was in the most agitated state. The clerk couldn't read a lot of it, and although she did ask from time to time, 'What does this say?' she didn't like to ask too often. She could see the state Mrs Bent was in and didn't want to do anything to make it worse. It worried her how bad she might get. Would she start shouting? Maybe even start banging about! She had seen that before. She had even seen Mrs Bent kick her handbag right across the room when she couldn't find something.

Mrs Bent's speech was now as unclear as her writing. She was starting the next sentence before she'd finished the last. She was thinking faster than she could talk. The clerk decided to type it out as best she could. It didn't matter if it was right or wrong - Mrs Bent didn't look at what she was signing.

Mrs Bent then went round to have it out with Elizabeth about the paper. Mrs Elders said that her claim about her daughter was a serious one – not just to say that she had been stealing but that she had been stealing from a charity. But Mrs Elders was 84 years old, so she had no voice. The more the two women denied it, the more determined Mrs Bent became. It made her very angry. How DARE they contradict her! She couldn't bear to have doubt put in her mind; it was dangerous, it made her feel threatened. She had to cling to her belief that it was Elizabeth, not her, who had been pilfering paper, and she had to remain free to blame her for it.

The next night she had another dream, the worst yet. She dreamed that people were surrounding her and telling her she wasn't normal. She was shrieking at them 'I am normal! I am!' and her throat began to hurt, she was shouting it so much. Then she saw two policemen coming slowly towards her. She knew what they were coming for - to put her away. Just when a fight was about to break out, she woke up and found herself sitting up in bed. She was in a dreadful sweat.

She realised she wasn't alone in the room.

'Are you all right Aunty?' her niece Maureen gently asked her. She had come to stay with her for a couple of days while visiting her old school friend.

'I'm fine' she tried to assure her, 'Go back to bed.' but she wasn't fine at all. She quietly got out of bed and went downstairs to make herself a cup of tea and ponder about it. The dream was wrong; she knew that. No such thing had ever happened to her. Then she began to think about Elizabeth. It was Elizabeth who had once had to be put away, she told herself.

The next day she went round to the Elders' home to find out more about this episode. Of course both she and her mother denied it, so Mrs Bent wrote in the notes, 'Date and circumstances unknown.' It was a mistake that took them three years to correct.

She also wrote, 'It has had a profound effect on her.' She was referring to the fact that Elizabeth kept denying it.

The next dream she had was more vivid still. It was one she couldn't remember properly afterwards, just cars, police cars, coming out of anywhere and whizzing about everywhere. She wasn't even certain if it was a roundabout they were going round and round. Nor did she know if she was a social worker in the dream, or where she was going.

It was five in the morning when she woke. She knew it would be impossible to go back to sleep, so she got up to make herself a cup of tea. As the clock slowly ticked away she thought more deeply into it. The night-time was so depressing, and it seemed morning would never come, yet there was one thing she did feel certain about - Elizabeth had to go. This nagging headache, this terrible nightmare, had now become a screaming one. It couldn't go on. Elizabeth had to be put away, right out of the way.

Still in a desperate state about it all, she went round to Elizabeth's the next morning. She needed to know what she was doing, what she could tell the doctors about her so that they would sign to have her committed. The two women, still not knowing to what extent she would refuse to investigate anything, were pleased to see her. They wanted to tell her they had more witnesses who had seen Paul Stalker and more character witnesses to say how capable they had always known Elizabeth to be. They couldn't have done a worse thing. They didn't know it was precisely because Elizabeth could manage so very well that Mrs Bent was so determined to take control of her life. Her ability to cope made her feel so inadequate.

Nor could Mrs Elders have done a worse thing than tell Mrs Bent she found it insulting to have someone talking about how well or how badly she was being looked after. 'I can look after myself' she would say, clearly getting worked up about it. Some people love to wind other people up - it gives them a buzz. Mrs Bent was one of them, and Sisley was another. It gave them a buzz to be patronizing, to say something like 'You are not as young as you used to be and have got to accept it that you need help.' They made her feel old and feeble. She hated it, but they knew what they were doing. In fact Mrs Elders suspected it. She once thought she detected a look of amusement on Mrs Bent's face,

Mrs Elders would say after she had been to the house, 'How dare this woman come round like this and criticise my daughter?' Yet she would manage to stay calm at the time, maybe because it bewildered her so much. Mrs Bent would say to her, 'You can't face up to this can you about your daughter?' and Mrs Elders, shaking her head in puzzlement, would ask 'Can't face up to what?'

Although Mrs Bent didn't believe in checking up on things, she did however look into the alleged compulsory admission into hospital. She asked Paul Stalker, who told her he had been there at the time, and that it had taken three of them to get Elizabeth into the yellow van. He was such a bad liar that he didn't even know what colour the van would have been.

She went round to Elizabeth's to have it out with her. Pointing a finger at her she said, 'Next time the ambulance comes for you, you are to get inside it and you are to get inside quietly.' But of course there had been no ambulance – she was making it up.

Elizabeth turned to her mother and said, 'You know what this means, don't you? It means she thinks the boys in the white coats have been for me.' Mrs Elders, finding it all very amusing said, 'Well I haven't seen any round here.' Then on seeing how serious Mrs Bent was about it all, standing there facing Elizabeth with her hands on her hips and scowling, she realised there was something very wrong. She shook her head in bewilderment.

'There's been no fight and no ambulance outside here' she said. But Mrs Bent wouldn't have it.

Meanwhile Paul Stalker was getting happier and happier as he became more and more convinced that Elizabeth would soon be certified and put into a mental hospital. People were getting hoax phone calls from him every twenty minutes. He was dialling any number he could get hold of, the window cleaner, the neighbours and so on, to try to get confidential details about Mrs Elder's financial affairs by pretending to be someone else. He wanted to know whether Mrs Elders had left anything in her will to anyone other than Elizabeth, whether anyone would be paying her rent in the new house she'd just bought, where the rents had gone for the house she'd just sold, and where had the money gone to when she sold it. One person said she felt her job was being threatened, he was phoning her up so much at work. She said he was phoning every ten minutes. 'Actually he's on the line now' she said. Mrs Elders said 'There's got to be an end to this. Only sixty people can say he's phoning them up every hour, and then they can only he kept them on for a minute.'

Something else had happened that had frightened them both very much and shocked everyone. It had put Elizabeth and her mother through a dreadful ordeal. Sisley had been talking very seriously about going to a Court of Protection to stop her mother from being able to sell her own house. By saying her mother didn't know what she was doing she could hold up the sale for months, by which time it might well fall through. Meanwhile Elizabeth and her mother would be forced to live in hell. They wouldn't have the money to move somewhere else.

Either Sisley didn't dare to follow this plan through or she didn't move fast enough. Mrs Elders' solicitor rushed it through, and the house was sold in three weeks.

It had been a big shock for the rest of the family to see the 'sold' notice up. Paul Stalker was especially put out by it, and he was determined to find out where they'd moved to. He started making phone calls to find out; he phoned one person and said, 'This is one of the furniture removal men here, please could you tell me Mrs Elders' new address, I need to deliver some furniture there.'

He thought the solicitor would be able to tell him something about the will. He said for example, 'Could you tell me please, has Mrs Elders left anything in it for the other daughter?' The solicitor couldn't be certain it was Paul Stalker speaking, but he was certain he had a crank on the other end of the line and he didn't paraphrase it when he told Elizabeth and her mother about it.

Paul Stalker was telling everyone that Elizabeth was very shortly going to be put into a mental institution and that the care of Mrs Elders would be given to him. He was talking as though it would be done through a court and the magistrates would make an order. One witness wrote in a letter, 'His claim was obviously nonsense and I could tell within a second that he would be most unsuitable for the job.'

Now they knew how Stalker thought he was going to get the money. Up until then Mrs Elders had always said, 'Even if I am found to be a dippy old woman and they come and put my daughter away, he's still not going to get it.' He was planning to sue Elizabeth for libel. Once he had won his case and Elizabeth had been ordered by a judge to pay him damages, Mrs Elders would have to give her daughter the money from the proceeds from the house to pay him out. Hence his interest in where the money had gone for the sale.

If only Mrs Bent would stop encouraging him with his dream that he was going to be able to sue Elizabeth. One witness wrote: '*I found his source of legal advice suspect. In fact I thought he was making unfounded statements with no legal advice at all. He said he hadn't been making a nuisance of himself round at the house and that it was slander for Elizabeth to say so.*'

Both Mrs Elders and Elizabeth continued to plead with Mrs Bent to get legal advice and to listen to what their own solicitor had said about it, but she claimed to believe they were imagining it. 'You don't realise do you how very serious this libel is?' she would tell them.

Elizabeth's solicitor was very serious when he heard some of the things Mrs Bent was telling the doctors about her. He knew they weren't true and feared they would do great damage. He telephoned her doctor to make certain he knew this too. He was especially concerned as he knew Mrs Bent was asking the doctors to section Elizabeth, and that it was also at the same time that both women were making out their wills. He very much feared that their family were getting ready to contest them. Yet it wasn't until later that it was confirmed what lies Mrs Bent was writing in her reports. It wasn't until later that the solicitor saw the director's letter in which she stated, wrongly, that Mrs Elders had dementia. It appeared the only thing Mrs Bent had checked up on was whether Elizabeth was vulnerable.

Elizabeth had made a big mistake in January 1992 in admitting that she had once had a nervous breakdown. She should have denied it and refused to tell them who her own doctor was. She was so stable at the time that she could easily have done this. Mrs Bent's idea of getting Elizabeth certified might have been a fantasy until that time, but now they were becoming more realistic. She was fast driving her victim into another nervous breakdown.

Chapter Four

SISLEY GETS TO WORK

Sisley was also getting carried away with ideas of what she would soon be able to do. She had no idea that a social worker couldn't say someone had dementia unless a doctor had diagnosed it, or that a social worker couldn't declare that a statement was libellous. In this case, Mrs Bent was behaving as though she was not just a lawyer but a judge. When Sisley's solicitor told her he couldn't do anything for her, she took it as a lovely surprise when a social worker told her she could.

Sisley and her husband had given it a try and Elizabeth and her mother had received a letter from their solicitor. It said that if Elizabeth had said anything that amounted to defamation of character, they wanted a complete withdrawal of the statement with a suitable apology. The letter also said that Sisley and Ronald had only ever done anything to help.

We already know what the couple's motive was here. By making this claim they could obtain quite a bit of power.

The letter finished with a subtle threat: 'We hope these matters can be settled amicably, as our clients have no wish to become embroiled in contentious litigation' it said.

Elizabeth's solicitor was very willing to write and say that she and her mother had the perfect defence – they hadn't done it. So it was brilliant news for Sisley when she was told that a social worker would see to it all for her.

Sometimes she would visualize Elizabeth in a mental hospital, looking miserable and yearning for freedom. She would be surrounded by doctors and social workers and the social workers would be standing with their hands on their hips, all scowling and all wearing white overalls. They would be asking her, 'Do you understand, this slander is very serious and you are NOT to say your brother-in-law was violent with you while your sister watched.' Elizabeth would be so desperate for freedom that she would simply be nodding her head in desperate agreement. 'I won't do it again, I won't do it again' she would be saying.

At other times Sisley would daydream about what would happen after they had let her out. Sisley would now be free to go inside the house as often as she liked, with no more letters from solicitors telling her she couldn't because a social worker would soon put a stop to those. She would now be able to order her sister to do anything, and if she didn't immediately jump to it then Ronald would be brought in. He would soon knock it into her that she had to comply. If Elizabeth dared to report any of this, they would soon be able to get her put away again. She would soon be retracting any statements she had made and pleading with them to let her out.

In fact the news was getting better and better. Sisley heard how parliament intended bringing in 'supervision orders' for people like Elizabeth. This would mean Social Services had more freedom to could come inside a patient's house and tell them what to do. They could make out a 'care plan' for people who especially needed supervising.

When Elizabeth heard about this she wrote to see what it was about and they sent her a document explaining it all. Of course, they claimed they were working in the patient's best interests. On the very first line it said the changes were 'to ensure the patient gets the care they need' and then went on to say what powers various people would be given and what force could be used. They could make her live in one particular place, and she would have to allow a supervisor or someone from the 'care team' into the house to make certain the plan was being followed. Mrs Bent was dreaming about being the supervisor and Sisley was dreaming about being a member of the care team.

Mrs Elders and Elizabeth talked about this at great length. In some ways you are at less risk in a mental hospital than in your own home. They weren't having social workers, care assistants or family members coming inside their house, and if the authorities did succeed in putting one of them away they weren't going to agree to this. They would always dream that one day they'd be able to go back home, to a home where they could be free.

Some people may be so bullied out in the community that they feel happier in a home. Elizabeth remembered a geriatric unit she had visited. The patients were put in a day room, and visitors were coming and going as though it was a drop-in centre. Nobody worried about enforcing visiting hours, because the carers knew that old people like to be near their families. There was a tea machine nearby and a canteen just round the corner. Elizabeth couldn't see there being much staff brutality going on there, but she could see plenty of it going on behind closed doors out in the community.

The last time Sisley had been to the house and her husband had been violent, she had been waving her hands about and giving orders. Elizabeth thought she was merely upset. She gently pointed at her and said, 'Don't do that', but Sisley kept shouting back 'I WILL do it, I WILL!' Now she believed she would have more freedom to do what she wanted.

The Elders had decided not to have a phone any more as the last bill had been so high and they had found it impossible to stop Paul Stalker using it, but Sisley had been insisting that they kept it. She and her husband were saying that no matter how high the bill was, no matter who ran it up, no matter who had to pay it (as long as it wasn't them), there had to be a phone.

Elizabeth did suggest that they should pay the latest bill, then consider whether or not to stay connected and how to stop Stalker using the phone. Elizabeth only suggested this as they had plenty of money. Yet not for a second would Sisley and Ronald consider it, even though at the same time they were making these big claims about caring for Mrs Elders and being so worried when they couldn't contact her.

There had been other times when Sisley and her husband had shown great meanness. They'd always made certain Mrs Elders paid for everything she wanted when they went out, down to a cup of tea. This was the mother who had always been so generous with them, always willing to do anything and to show them how happy she was to do it, and compared with them she was poor. They were making her pay for everything, yet Mrs Bent was planning on giving them power over her.

After Ronald was violent with Elizabeth, they both spoke gently to Mrs Elders. They explained to her that she could now have a phone. They had dealt with it for her. They made out that Elizabeth was a dreadful bully who she lived in fear of, but they had now rescued her.

Sisley didn't try to use the pets to control her mother, a well-known way of doing it, but she did try to use her children. She believed that because it was she who had married and had a family of her own, and Mrs Elders had always adored them, she had the advantage over Elizabeth. Up to a point Elizabeth had believed this too, though it was quite wrong. It amazed her when her mother immediately accepted that she couldn't see them any more. She said,

'If this is the price I have to pay then I will just have to go without seeing the children.' Was fear stronger than love, or was it her determination for justice? It would indeed be unfair if she had been swayed, because Elizabeth had no other family and Sisley had such a big one. In fact, it was shortly after Elizabeth's husband had been violent that another great-grandson was born.

It had been something of a relief to Elizabeth that her mother wasn't going to be swayed by her sister's advantage, but it was a big disappointment to Sisley. Yet it did mean she had one more thing to blame Elizabeth for. She was spreading it about that Elizabeth was greatly intimidating her 'old and feeble' mother by forbidding her to see any of her grandchildren or great-grandchildren. She was putting it all down to mental health problems. She just said 'She's a schizophrenic', as if that explained everything.

It was true that Elizabeth had once been diagnosed with schizophrenia, but that had been a long time ago, and it was a poor diagnosis. She had always been in touch with reality. She had never been unduly paranoiac. Only one doctor had called it schizophrenia. It didn't make any difference what treatment she had. In fact the only thing that did matter was the stigma. Schizophrenia isn't what a lot of people think it is. Often the sufferers remain quiet and withdrawn; only the worst cases reach the papers. Violence isn't usually involved, and when a schizophrenic is violent it is usually only because of drugs or alcohol.

At that time Sisley was confident that should an expert witness be brought in a slander case he would say something like, 'These neurotic women dream it up sometimes that a man has assaulted them', though an expert witness might have said something quite different. He might have said that people with mental health problems are vulnerable and get attacked more often than they attack someone else, and that this was a typical case of abuse. Yet Sisley, not knowing any of this, remained very confident that she would be seen simply as the dedicated daughter who soldiered on. She had a sister to see to with schizophrenia and a mother with Alzheimer's Disease. It was such nonsense! For a start people with Alzheimer's do not necessarily turn aggressive, but in any case, her mother simply didn't have it. A Social Services diagnosis of dementia had grown in the telling. It was also found out later that Sisley's husband had telephoned the psychiatrist and said, 'Elizabeth needs help'. He had asked him to section her.

Sisley thought it would be accepted that you have to be cruel to be kind, and when she decided to take over her mother's life she didn't intend to do it gently. She had the most authoritarian approach. For example, on the day Mrs Elders forbade her to contact Social Services about her, she not only telephoned them but spoke to her mother very sharply about it, saying she was going to do so anyway. She was making the claim of course that she was only doing so because she cared about her so much. This was of course fully supported by Mrs Bent.

It was thoroughly dangerous that Sisley was willing to give such support to Paul Stalker. If his mad telephone calls and crazy allegations were going to be followed by a phone call from someone like Sisley to back them up, the doctors might fear there was some truth in them and that they might be sued. Sisley was good at sounding sincere and well-intentioned. Elizabeth feared that a doctor would especially fear being sued and would give Sisley and Paul Stalker the benefit of the doubt, as they were both family and both clearly had money of their own.

Mrs Bent was planning on returning to the house with Sisley after Elizabeth had been taken away and telling Mrs Elders that she and Elizabeth had lost their rights over one another and that Social Services were now in control and with Sisley, they would be taking the place over. They would have control over Mrs Elders' life in her own home, as well as power over Elizabeth.

Mrs Bent had sat in the front room refusing to leave. Elizabeth had asked her several times 'Please will you leave?', but she would not. Elizabeth wanted to get her coat, go out herself and hope that when she came back she would be gone, but she didn't dare. She suspected that Mrs Bent, not Paul Stalker, had been moving things around, even hiding them, to make her think she was mad when she couldn't find them.

'Can your sister come round here?' Mrs Bent asked Elizabeth. It was one more mad thing she said. 'No!' Elizabeth shrieked. 'She'll bring her husband with her and he's already been violent with me once.'

'But she IS your sister' replied Mrs Bent.

'What is that supposed to mean?' asked Elizabeth. She didn't know that Mrs Bent was preparing to tell her that she had no right to say she wasn't having her in the house, and that while being forcibly held in hospital she would be forced to accept her sister inside the house. The reason given would be the welfare of Mrs Elders, as well as her own.

Elizabeth kept quietly asking Mrs Bent to go, but she refused every time. These days this would be a criminal offence, because Elizabeth would be protected by the Harassment Act 1997. The police could be called. They could warn Mrs Bent, or even caution her. None of the reasons given for her visit were valid.

She said Elizabeth had written to the headmaster of a local school, but Mrs Bent had guessed what the letter had said and had got it completely wrong. She also said she had been acting upon delusion, which she had not. Yet Mrs Bent herself continued to act upon her own false and very fixed beliefs.

Maybe strangest of all, Mrs Bent noted that Elizabeth was consistent with what she said. She wrote, 'Word for word the same'.

Yet it didn't seem to cross her mind that Elizabeth was so consistent because she was telling the truth.

So Mrs Bent continued to sit in Elizabeth's front room, refusing to leave. Elizabeth went away to make herself a cup of tea, telling her mother to stay where she was. She didn't tell her she feared that Mrs Bent might start messing about with some of her belongings if she was left alone.

When she came back, Mrs Bent was still sitting there. When she was questioned later about this, she said she had been asked to do an assessment on Elizabeth's mental health and had to complete it. She omitted to say that it had been requested by Paul Stalker, and the authorities overlooked the fact that her response was in breach of the Mental Health Act 1983. According to the Act, the nearest relative is the only relative who can ask for such a thing.

It seems there was hysteria on the subject of libel. According to Mrs Bent another social worker also requested an assessment. According to a letter written in the notes this man stated that he was concerned about Elizabeth's ability to care for her mother. He may not have said this at all, and in any case she didn't have to do what he said, especially as it was she who was qualified in mental health.

Unfortunately though, as Elizabeth could clearly manage so well, the letter aroused suspicion. It made some people think he was worried that he was not qualified to care for old people and was leaving the responsibility to Elizabeth. Those who knew him didn't think so – they said he was a good social worker - but it did make them wonder if he thought he should be doing something about Mrs Bent, and it was this that he transferred.

Elizabeth wrote in her diary at one point: 'Social worker says there is an enormous amount of concern', but she didn't say which social worker said it or what the concern was about. Maybe she was too afraid to know. Maybe she feared it too much, as there was hysteria going around the place on the subject of libel.

There was also an enormous amount of concern about Mrs Bent. But on this day, when Mrs Bent finally did decide to go, it was tempting for Elizabeth to give her a bit of a push to help her on her way out of the front door. And then Mrs Bent did stop to have one last go at her. She stood in the hall and really began to rattle. It was a monologue of absolute piffle. 'You have a good sister who really cares for you!' she rattled on. Elizabeth wanted to put her hands over her ears to keep out the noise. She just would not stop. She wanted to cry out, 'Shurrup, shurrup, SHURRUP!'

Elizabeth had no idea at the time how dangerous this all was, what the motive might be, or how hard someone would fight for power. She didn't know either that by making the claim that she believed all this, Mrs Bent might be able to help Sisley to get quite a bit of control, which could mean that in turn Mrs Bent would get it.

Elizabeth, very upset, exclaimed, 'Never come round to this house again!', but Mrs Bent strolled away without a care in the world. Those who know the Mental Health Act will know why.

After Mrs Bent claimed that Sisley's interest was in them, Elizabeth went upstairs to tell her mother. Mrs Elders was already running round and round the room screaming 'That bloody, bloody social worker!' But now she started waving her arms about, screaming 'The audacity of it all! I've known my daughter all her life, she's hardly met her and she says she knows her better than I do!'

Elizabeth calmed her down with a cup of tea and a piece of cake, reassuring her that she had really put her foot down this time. Mrs Bent had gone and the nightmare was over. They could now forget about it all and she wouldn't be round again. This was very naive of Elizabeth.

Mrs Bent soon came round again, this time with a psychiatrist. She was so keen to have his support that she gave him her own private home number and was anxiously hanging about the phone at home waiting for his answer. Would he or wouldn't he section Elizabeth for her? The load it would take off her would be enormous. It would sign all her troubles away. No more feeling guilty - she would be free from all blame at last! By sectioning Elizabeth he would confirm for her that Elizabeth was to blame for it all. She never felt so certain that she had chosen the right job.

She continued to dream about having more and more power. Maybe after having cleared the field of Elizabeth and making it clear to Mrs Elders she now had control over her in her own home, she could get even more power over Elizabeth. She could visit her in hospital, talk to her in a kind voice, ask her if she wanted anything, go out to the shops and get it for her. But this would only last a very short time. As Elizabeth deteriorated and came to terms with her situation she would have to stay there. Mrs Bent would then become very stern. She hoped that the hospital staff would be stern too, and that she would be given a chance to support them.

Elizabeth was meanwhile in a dreadful state about the psychiatrist turning up like that. He had travelled eight miles to see her. It had to be a doctor who knew her, so he came from where she used to live. Mrs Bent called it an 'urgent' visit, though the only emergency was that Paul Stalker had been slandered. She wrote it in the report.

Maybe most of all Elizabeth minded the psychiatrist seeing what a mess her house had got into. Apart from it being very embarrassing and making her feel like a slut, she knew it was a symptom of mental illness. Anyone's house would get into a mess with moving, but this was one she couldn't get out of. She was in too much of a dither to be able to manage it all, and she realised the social worker was driving her into a nervous breakdown.

The psychiatrist asked her if she was sleeping at night. She wasn't. Due to all this she had suffered dreadful insomnia, but it was a dangerous question to have to answer. The night is a dangerous time.

It's when people try to commit suicide, and they can put you away for that. He knew she had already made one serious attempt, though it had been fifteen years ago. She had gone into an empty room and begun to swallow tablets. She swallowed and swallowed. She was going, going... her head started to spin. She began falling around the room and finally collapsed into a chair. Forever – as she thought. But what was this? There were voices all around her. They were calling her name. Three days had passed and she had woken up in the Intensive Care Unit at the hospital.

Yet all that was such a long time ago. She hoped it would be seen as ancient history. The psychiatrist's opinion was based on facts, a solicitor checked them up. He had prescribed her something to calm her down. He knew she had been constantly harassed. If he had prescribed it on the grounds that she was deluded, as Mrs Bent had told him she was, then she would have been referred to an expert in slander. It would mean that what she had said had done damage, especially as Elizabeth turned out to be sensitive to the drug he put her on. According to Mrs Bent he told her Elizabeth was deluded. If he did, he was nagged into agreeing to it.

The psychiatrist had been receiving a few strange calls himself. He suspected they were fake, but by the time Elizabeth asked him about it his memory was pretty vague. As a psychiatrist he was used to having a crank on the other end of the line, so he was less likely to remember.

The following evening, as Mrs Bent got into her car to go home, her thoughts were distracting her. Her mind was still racing away when she realised she was fast approaching a crossroads. She braked hard and went into a skid, the car spinning round. Another car was coming towards her and swerved to miss her. She finished up on the pavement next to the wall. Realising that no damage seemed to have been done, she breathed a sigh of relief. Only one person had seen the incident, and he had gone.

Then she saw a police car driving slowly towards her. 'Stay calm, don't panic' she told herself, wondering if someone had reported something. The police car drove on; they hadn't.

It was seven in the evening when she found herself tapping on Elizabeth's front window. Why had she done that? She went round to knock on the front door instead. She couldn't think what she was doing there. It was as though she had sleepwalked to the house.

'What, you again?' said Elizabeth angrily when she answered it. 'Now what is it?'

'Nothing much' Mrs Bent said meekly. 'I just want to know if you are allowed to drive a car.'

'Just leave me alone!' shouted Elizabeth. Mrs Bent strolled thoughtfully away. Her own actions worried her. 'What did I do that for?' she asked herself.

Elizabeth watched her going down the drive, which curved round for a good fifty yards to a big gateway. She strolled slowly away, as though in a world of her own, and for the first time in her life Elizabeth felt some pity for the woman. It was the walk of a very sad person. Clearly there was something deeply wrong with Mrs Bent.

Elizabeth had a very bad dream that night. She dreamed she was sitting at the back of a bus, getting away from everything, but as the bus drove faster and faster and she was getting further and further away, she was getting more and more bewildered. She had lost her memory. When she awoke she knew the writing was on the wall. She had to act fast, but at the same time she was to take care. She must not have a nervous breakdown. Losing her memory would be dreadful, it would mean she wouldn't even recognise her own mother, but that was only one kind of nervous breakdown. Take care, she thought – take care.

Mrs Bent continued to believe anything Paul Stalker said, regardless of how bizarre it was or how many witnesses there were to contradict him. He complained that Elizabeth was phoning him the whole of the time and that he was finding it a thorough nuisance. She spoke to Elizabeth extremely seriously about it, telling her it had to stop. She did not accept that Elizabeth had never phoned him, even once.

This caused great anxiety among people who knew Elizabeth. They could see it was having an effect on her and they feared it would make her believe that she had made the calls. One man told her how a woman had kept accusing him of continually telephoning her, until eventually he began to ask himself if he had.

Elizabeth didn't believe she was doing all these mad, crazy things, but she began to believe Mrs Bent had a point. She believed she had never really got over her nervous breakdown, and that an eye had to be kept on her. They managed to brainwash her into believing this.

They continued to talk about her 'libel' against Paul Stalker as though it was a murder she had committed. They spoke to her far more seriously about it than the hospital had done fifteen years before, when she had tried to kill herself. She began to think she was going mad again. She saw herself becoming hysterical, jumping over walls, running away, and people looking out of their windows and saying, 'That woman is truly mad!' In fact they were emphasising it, telling her she was sane, and that if Mrs Bent knocked on the door she should not answer it.

Mrs Bent wrote in the report: 'Pleaded with Elizabeth not to write any more letters'. She continued to behave as though she was some kind of judge. She forbade Elizabeth to take a solicitor's advice. Yet for her even to write that, to say, 'pleaded with', did at least show one thing - that she did sometimes pause for a second to think about what she was saying.

Yet should she even be doing that? Should she have merely pleaded with Elizabeth about it? It was greatly interfering with family matters, and getting far more into legal ones. It had nothing to do with Elizabeth's health. Yet it should be added that the conversation was a very confused one. She was in such a dither on the subject of libel that it made it very difficult for Elizabeth to know what she was saying, and impossible for her to know what she really meant to say. In fact, she might not have known herself.

If the letters had been libellous, if Stalker's threats to sue Elizabeth had been realistic and if her mental health really had been deteriorating, it would have been for a social worker to see that she got proper legal advice, not contradict her solicitor.

On this occasion, it was practically impossible for Elizabeth to even start what she was saying, never mind finish it. Mrs Bent just kept throwing her hands up and shouting 'No! No! No!'. Elizabeth was trying to say that she couldn't promise not to write any more letters, as her solicitor might advise her to write one. He might want to write on her behalf, if the brother-in-law was violent with her again. Did Mrs Bent know what she was saying 'no' to? If so, why did she want to put a stop to it? Did she think the solicitor might write something libellous and it was her duty to prevent it?

She also said she had reassured Paul Stalker that she had told Elizabeth not to write any more letters about him. Elizabeth was very shocked. She was well aware how out of order it was for her to do that. She tried to explain this to Mrs Bent, but she just sat there saying that they did have the right, and Elizabeth was not to do it.

Stalker told Mrs Bent that Elizabeth had phoned him up and said 'I'm God, so I can do whatever I like'. This was to imply that she could be deluded and dangerous and should be put away. Mrs Bent told Elizabeth it was his word against hers and she didn't know which one to believe. Elizabeth was gobsmacked that Mrs Bent believed Elizabeth could think she was God.

Later Elizabeth discovered that while it was her word against his, it was she who should have been given the benefit of the doubt, as she had the good character witnesses and he the bad ones. Yet it was he who was believed. Mrs Bent told the psychiatrist that Elizabeth was calling herself God, but she failed to mention that this report had come from a notorious liar.

It had come as a great relief to Mrs Bent that Stalker had made this allegation. She had had another bad dream, yet this time it was one of hope. She saw again the elderly woman with her hair tied back in a bun. The woman spoke to her in a kind and gentle voice and told her she had delusions of grandeur and that as a social worker this made her dangerous. Mrs Bent wanted to cry, put her hand out to the woman, wanted to touch her and to ask her for some comfort, but then she woke up with a jolt. It was a relief the next morning to receive a phone call from Paul Stalker and hear him say that Elizabeth had delusions of grandeur and that they could make her dangerous. In fact she had asked him only a few days ago if he had seen any signs of this. He told her he couldn't remember anything, but now that he was able to tell her this she felt enormously relieved.

The day Elizabeth wrote in her diary 'Mrs Bent made a vicious attack on me today', Mrs Bent went rushing off to tell a psychiatrist that her sister had complained about her, saying she was malicious. But Mrs Elders had said throughout it all, 'Everything with her is back to front.'

* * * * * * * *

As regards Paul Stalker's threats to sue Elizabeth for libel, despite the monologue Mrs Bent was giving on the subject, Elizabeth managed to say that it didn't matter if he did as she would have someone in court to defend her. Mrs Bent said she wouldn't. It wasn't until much later that Elizabeth found out what she meant by that. She meant that all the witnesses she claimed she had would turn out to be fictional; hence the defending counsel would be standing there helpless.

The subject of libel continued to obsess Mrs Bent. She had to find someone to accuse of it. Sometimes she would sit there in silence for a long time worrying, and at others she would be worked up in the most excited state. One day when she was worked up, she made a couple of assumptions. Although Elizabeth had tried to explain to her that libel was a civil offence and not a criminal one, and therefore not a police matter, her mind was racing ahead too fast for her to be take this in. Convinced that Elizabeth's letters were libel and that this was common knowledge, she assumed Paul Stalker's neighbours believed the same thing. Naming the wrong police station, she wrote in her report, 'The letters, being libellous, were forwarded to the police'. Elizabeth tried to tell her differently and to get her to understand that the letters had been forwarded to the police station for a completely different reason - because the neighbours knew other things about him which were a police matter.

After this Mrs Bent wrote, 'Elizabeth says that if the police take her to court then people will finally hear the truth about Paul Stalker'. Elizabeth had not said that. She said nothing about the police. She knew that Paul Stalker could try to take out a libel action against her, but it wouldn't be the police.

Nor did she say the truth would 'finally' come out, as claimed by Mrs Bent, who had heard what she wanted to hear. Her false beliefs were completely fixed. She assumed Elizabeth was getting more and more frustrated because no one would believe her. She was totally unaware that she was the only one who was saying that Elizabeth had delusions.

Everyone was mystified. In fact if it had gone to court the truth might have come out about her. An expert witness could have been brought, a psychologist, and a court might have accepted what they said.

Yet how fixed were her delusions? Although she wrote in the report that Elizabeth had them, which would suggest to some people she did, she was only acting upon them up to a point. It wasn't that she was speaking to witnesses and despite anything they told her she still went on saying it. It was that she refused to speak to them at all. It wasn't that she got legal advice, and despite anything a lawyer said she still went on insisting it was libel. It was that she refused to get any legal advice at all. It was different from another case, the one where social workers were so certain of witchcraft, Satan and worshipping the devil, when they were so determined something dangerous was going on and their beliefs were so very strong that they continued their campaign through the high court. It was a campaign they lost dismally.

Much later, both Mrs Bent and her team leader told the Social Services Complaints Officer that they were afraid Stalker might carry out his threats to sue Elizabeth for libel. This wasn't because they were both so honest. They could both tell a lie all right. It was because they didn't know how strange it was. However, it did suggest that Mrs Bent knew that only a civilian can do this. Remember she wouldn't have her mind racing away with her when talking to him. It would be completely different with a Complaints Officer. Yet even then, if she did make any mention of the police to him, he would soon put her right on that. A Complaints Officer would never let her make herself look so silly as to say, 'Sued by the police by libel'.

Chapter Five

LOOPING

Elizabeth now became a victim of what some people call 'looping', or twisting people's words against them. That is, the very thing you say to try to prove your case is used to undo you and prove your opponent is right. When Paul Stalker started phoning everyone up every ten minutes, including Social Services, instead of saying, 'Doesn't it show what the Elders have had to put up with?' they said, 'Doesn't it show how mad she's driven him, doesn't it show how right he is when he says we should deal with her for him?'

One social worker said sympathetically, 'he's very upset'. They said he couldn't be blamed for his 'explosion' (their word) after what she had done to him. They did not accept what he was really like. Nor did they accept that he would never keep to an agreement and that force would have to be used. It was only after the police came down very heavily that he was stopped. In fact it was largely because of cases like this that the Protection from Harassment Act 1997 was passed, followed by the Human Rights Act.

Why did Elizabeth bother to give examples of his behaviour when they were so convinced he was telling the truth? Yet she did. The first was about a girl he had once stalked. He had been seeking revenge because she had left him and her father had been round to the house about it. Paul Stalker agreed to leave her alone for a month, but he didn't even keep his promise for an afternoon – he was round there within hours. That was a big disappointment to a lot of people, as it had been hoped that he would forget her in that month. It was an especially big disappointment to the girl's father. He had been quite pleased with himself for, as he thought, reasoning successfully with him. He did not know how easily some people can agree to something, with no intention of keeping their promise.

Another girl telephoned Mrs Elders in tears. She had taken the morning off work to see a solicitor and had asked him to write Stalker a letter telling him not to go round to the house any more. He had gone to the house the day he received it. The Elders were sorry the girl hadn't told them about the letter, because they could have told her he would ignore it and saved her a lot of time and money. She had lost a morning's pay as well as having to pay the solicitor's bill. But Social Services refused to accept any of this. They continued to blame Elizabeth for everything.

People who were fully in the picture - a lodger, two neighbours and a close friend – agreed with Elizabeth that the most extraordinary claim Social Services made was about the effect their handling had had on Stalker. They claimed it had been their gentle, tactful handling of him that had stopped him coming to the house. Of course it was the rough handling by the police down at the police station that same day that had done the job. They claimed the timing was just a coincidence. They did not accept that no one had been able to do a thing with him since the day he was born.

This was one more shock Elizabeth felt unable to stand up to. It was like being kicked after falling downstairs.

'We should let the police know how deluded Social Services are' said Mrs Elders. 'We should let them know that they are accusing them of wasting their time that day down at the police station and that they should have left him to them.'

The police were being accused of having the most appalling judgement. Maybe they did have the right to know that this was being said about them, but there was a much bigger point. It would have been confirmation for them that Social Services were completely over the top with their views about themselves and something was very wrong. It was in the public interest that the police should be told, as they work so closely to them. However, they might be taking, Elizabeth said, too much of a risk 'criticising one uniform to another'.

Social Services told Elizabeth, 'You're entitled to your views and we're entitled to ours'. Maybe that's correct, but should they be social workers if they have opinions as strange as that? They can do a lot of damage. They have such a lot of power with their opinions.

There should be an easy, straightforward way of stopping the authorities getting opinion mixed up with fact. For example, with the issue of whether Paul Stalker was harassing them, or whether or not the woman next door said 'Tell those social workers to come and see me if they say he wasn't there' - that's fact, not opinion.

However, it was Elizabeth's opinion that Mrs Bent was the biggest fool ever when she had said they would be able to put a stop to Stalker's phone calls by sending him a letter on headed notepaper. Did she actually believe he would take any notice of that? Elizabeth yearned to be free to scream at her, 'YOU bloody fool YOU!' He had had plenty such letters before from solicitors and others, but they had all gone straight into the bin. This was before the Harassment Act or the Human Rights Act. It showed that Mrs Bent had no understanding of the dreadful nightmare Stalker had put Elizabeth and her mother through.

It also showed that she did not accept that they had tried every possible peaceful means of getting rid of him before it had come to this. In fact, she appeared to be in denial, unable to accept anything

Elizabeth said. If a letter on headed notepaper would have worked, Elizabeth would have got a solicitor to send one a long time ago. The police had been round to the house about him several times, asking how they could lock him up. They had questioned both Elizabeth and her mother to see if he'd done anything that enabled them to do so. They also talked about an injunction, but they were well aware that the only way to stop Paul Stalker was to put him in a police cell.

Mrs Bent saying a letter on headed notepaper would stop him reminded Elizabeth of what another idiot had once said to her about a dangerous man buying a car. She had said it would be OK because he wouldn't be able to pass his driving test. She imagined first that he would bother to take the test and second, that if he did take it and failed it he wouldn't drive, and that would keep him off the roads. But that person wasn't a social worker, so she wasn't expected to know any better. Mrs Bent was.

One day when Stalker had been harassing Elizabeth outside a corner shop, she ran all the way home. Some teenage boys in school uniform helped to chase him away. She hoped they would be witnesses to it, so she wrote to the school saying how helpful they'd been and thanking them. Unfortunately this got back to Mrs Bent, and she was very angry. She went round to the house to have it out with Elizabeth. 'What else am I going to find out about you!' she cried, throwing her hands up.

At that time the Elders didn't know that Mrs Bent lived in fear of her own weaknesses being discovered. It was only later they found out that this incident had nothing to do with her and that she was saying it didn't take place. The word she used in the report was 'delusional' – it was almost as if she was saying that Elizabeth had been hallucinating. It was also later found out that Mrs Bent hadn't seen the letter to the school and had only guessed what it said. Her guess could not have been more to the contrary. She wrote that

Elizabeth had written complaining about the boys and saying that they had been being a nuisance near her home.

It wasn't that she was criticising everything Elizabeth was doing - it was that she was saying she had done things which she hadn't. Elizabeth also feared that Stalker would take an overdose and she'd be blamed for it. He'd taken them before. He'd immediately go and tell someone he'd done it, and then say later, 'You know what happened to me don't you?' He would talk as though he was an innocent victim. He would talk about whose fault it was, because it was never his own.

Mrs Bent asked Elizabeth, 'Do you feel you would like to harm your sister in some way for this, would you like to hurt her?' Elizabeth's blood ran cold. She knew what she was trying to show, that Elizabeth might be a threat to her sister with her 'false' beliefs. Nothing could have been more to the contrary. It was she who was threatened by Sisley.

As Mrs Bent was leaving Elizabeth walked a little way down the drive with her. She pointed at some flats next door and said, 'Go and talk to the people there, I can see they're in, they have agreed to be witnesses.' But Mrs Bent wouldn't go. She just went on writing in the report that it was all 'delusional'.

Plenty of people wanted to help Elizabeth. For example, two men said they'd been receiving strange phone calls from Paul Stalker. They commented that he was out to get her and wanted to reassure her that she wasn't being unduly paranoiac. In a letter for her solicitor, they said, 'His tone was unfriendly and very suspicious, we suspected he was intent on causing her stress'. They'd been more than willing to tell Mrs Bent, but again she didn't want to know. She wanted Elizabeth and her mother to behave like lunatics, and that's exactly what she got. Now they had the curtains drawn all day, hardly daring to peep round them to see who might be approaching the house. When they were out on the street they took care to keep their voices down.

* * * * * * * *

A young French woman called Maria had been living in the house. One day when she had returned from a visit to France and no one else was in, she let Mrs Bent into the house to talk to her. She wanted to stick up for Elizabeth. She wanted to say that although she had been living in the house for six years, she had seen Sisley so infrequently that she didn't recognise her when she did come. She told Mrs Bent that Sisley never did a thing to help - everything was always left to Elizabeth. But more than that, she wanted to make it clear about Paul Stalker. 'She's had a dreadful time with this cousin of hers' she told Mrs Bent. But Mrs Bent, not accepting any of this, still challenged her by asking 'Yes, but have you actually seen him?'.

This made Maria's blood run cold. She realised that Mrs Bent was suggesting that Elizabeth had been hallucinating. She was horrified. Surely a social worker could not be as deluded as that?

Maria wondered if Paul Stalker had given money to Mrs Bent. It reminded her of another incident some years before when a neighbour had accused her of going into her home when she was out. The neighbour's delusions were so severe that she had had all the locks on her doors changed. The woman clung on to her beliefs in the face of all the evidence, just as Mrs Bent was doing now.

Quietly Maria said to Mrs Bent, 'Indeed I have seen him, very frequently, and so have a lot of other people including another lodger who's been living in the house'. But Mrs Bent wouldn't have it. After this she wrote in the report about it, all contradicting Maria.

She had also said to Maria 'I thought everything was all right until I heard she was doing all this'. She made it sound as though it had all been confirmed by someone reliable, but of course she had heard it from Paul Stalker.

Maria turned round to Elizabeth, and looking very wide eyed, as though she was ready for a shock, she asked 'What have you been DOING?' But she should have put that question to Mrs Bent. Just what was going on in her mind? Yet Elizabeth answered Maria's question calmly. 'I promise you I have told you everything' she said. 'You know the whole truth.'

Maria had also asked Mrs Bent about the compulsory admission into hospital she was planning for Elizabeth. She wanted to know what she was thinking of. She asked how long it would take and was told it could take a week or as little as a day. That made Maria's blood run cold again. She realised how determined Mrs Bent was. Why was she doing it? She wondered again if money was involved; maybe the sister had promised her something. She frequently said later, 'There's money somewhere here, if only at the back of her mind'. She knew very little about psychologists and did not know that they would come up very quickly with another explanation.

Yet would a psychologist wonder if Mrs Bent thought she might get some money out of this, if only as a secondary motive? They were certain it was a power thing in the case of Dr Shipman, yet he was stealing off his victims as well as murdering them.

Maria also found it ironic that Mrs Bent wrote, 'Elizabeth has now acted upon her delusions' and then went on to demonstrate how she herself was acting upon her own. For example, she sent a community psychiatric nurse round to the house to check her mental health. There comes a time when to say someone is acting upon delusions is deluded in itself.

The night of Mrs Bent's conversation with Maria, Elizabeth came home in a dreadful state about it all. Maria grabbed her at the door, and then, pleadingly, as though she was on her knees to her, said,

'Where are you going to in this dreadful state? Whatever this woman tells you to do, do it and get out of Grimley within a week. I mean it, they're coming to put you away!'

Early next morning at about six o'clock there was a quiet knock on the door. Mrs Elders and Elizabeth didn't know whether to run straight out of the back door or creep out, but then a soft voice said, 'It's only me'. It was a neighbour who had been down to the library to look a few things up. He had laughed when he was told the authorities could come inside your house and take you away, but now he was very serious. He knew they could. The Elders spent quite a bit of time reassuring him that Elizabeth did have somewhere safe to go to, and that very soon she would be there.

Elizabeth knew that when a woman is mad she can hallucinate strongly and believe a man is persecuting her. She will cry out in desperation 'He is, he is, he is!' So Elizabeth didn't do that - she knew it would be behaving too much like a typical madwoman. But she did try desperately hard to get her to check up on all the many witnesses she had. A woman who is hallucinating doesn't have witnesses. She said 'Ask Tom, ask Harry, ask Terry'. She wouldn't ask any of her neighbours, or any of the workmen who saw Paul Stalker going off with their mail, saying he always dealt with the Elders' post.

She wouldn't check with the people whose house he went round to and said, 'I'm allowed to have the key to the house' - their twelve-year-old boy gave it to him. She wouldn't ask the removal men who found him such a nuisance when moving some of their stuff, or their manager, who spoke to a solicitor on the phone about it. The list of witnesses went on and on, but Mrs Bent wouldn't have any of it. All delusional, she said.

Neighbours continued to try to help. They still had records of how often they had seen Paul Stalker and for how long. When they were told Social Services weren't interested, but had said it would be all right because a tribunal would listen to her 10-21 days after they'd had her committed, they hid her away. They reassured both Elizabeth and her mother that when the ambulance came the crew wouldn't be able to find her. It was typical arrogance on the part of Social Services. They had no doubt that everyone would say 'if those social workers say she should go, she should go'. In fact they were saying 'Those social workers don't half need a kick up the backside'.

But the ambulance never came. Every day the news was the same – no one had seen it. Elizabeth's solicitor telephoned her doctor and established that it was not going to come. It hadn't been realistic for Social Services to think they were going to get a doctor to sign.

Elisabeth later found out that even if they had succeeded, she still might not have had to wait day in and day out in agony for a tribunal to come round. In a case like this there can be an alternative remedy - to apply to the High Court. If it can be shown that a social worker's actions were arbitrary, carried out in bad faith, or there was evidence of malicious harassment prior to admission, this sort of application can be heard more quickly. Yet even though Elizabeth had a wealth of evidence to put forward, and even though she was vulnerable, there was no chance of anyone knowing what would have happened if a doctor had signed because there was never any chance that one would.

This is how a neighbour described in a letter the effect all this had on Elizabeth:

"Elizabeth leads a full and active life in addition to being a sincere, warm and honest individual. About twelve months ago, my husband and I noticed she had changed from her usual cheerful self to an unhappy, agitated and frightened person. Upon further investigation, we discovered the reason for her deterioration was because certain members of her family, i.e. Paul Stalker, her sister and her brother-in-law, were taking an aggressive and mercenary interest in her mother's estate. I can categorically assure you that what she is claiming is fundamentally factual

and true. There's no doubt whatsoever, Paul Stalker sustained a campaign of intimidation, intrusion against Elizabeth and her mother in a calculated and relentless fashion. I am certain that the reason for this was to discredit Elizabeth and undermine the special relationship she holds with her mother. Thus leaving the field clear to persuade Mrs Elders to change her will in his favour.

That letter went on to name three other witnesses. Elizabeth was a victim of misogyny, domestic violence, and the greed of relatives whose only interest was in the family inheritance, yet a social worker had taken their side.

When she came out of hiding she had to go into hospital, to have two major operations and a minor one. Stress takes down one's resistance, and while she had survived mentally, she had not done so well physically. It is well known that carers are more likely to be ill than other people. She believed that if Social Services had given support to her and her mother instead of to Paul Stalker, none of her operations would have been necessary. Yet she had been offered no support whatsoever. For example, she wasn't told about group therapy, a place where carers can get together to talk about their problems, nor about Women's Aid, which gives support to victims of domestic violence.

When she asked to see her notes they were horrendous, far worse than she had ever imagined. She now knew just how much Mrs Bent had taken the side of Sisley and Ronald against her. As far as they were concerned Elizabeth was someone who needed to be very harshly treated. She was one of those neurotic and dangerous women who dream it up that a man has assaulted her and is persecuting her. She wasn't a victim of harassment at all. Mrs Bent had rubbished everything that Elizabeth had told her. Before she saw the notes Elizabeth had only had her suspicions, but now she knew for sure.

Yet it was all very strange. Mrs Bent had written 'Elizabeth becomes agitated and on the defensive when she realises her mental health may be an issue'. Then a bit later, 'Elizabeth is highly suspicious of any suggestion relating to mental health'.

She would not consider for a second that perhaps Elizabeth was right, perhaps there was nothing wrong with her and perhaps she was just someone vulnerable being picked upon.

However it explained a lot. For example, Mrs Elders and Elizabeth had once said that they would contact Social Services in the area where Paul Stalker lived. They would be different social workers. Mrs Bent said a colleague of hers had told her they wouldn't even go round to his house to see him about it. Elisabeth and her mother were mystified. The social workers would be round at the house at the least little complaint he made about them.

Now they knew. He would indeed have Mrs Bent to defend him. She would be willing to say he was being slandered and that his rights for privacy should be respected. Yet Mrs Bent had already explained all this to Elizabeth following a complaint he had made that Elisabeth had been trying to find out who his doctor was. She had not. It was one more lie he had told. But Mrs Bent accepted what he said and not what Elizabeth said. Elizabeth became more and more amazed at how eager she was to stick up for him, sounding angry. Mrs Bent told her 'People feel threatened, why should you know who his doctor is?'

Mrs Bent didn't take Elizabeth's complaint about Stalker seriously - that he had got the key to the house by deception, let himself in when he knew no one would be there, looked through Elizabeth's papers to find out who her psychiatrist was and was phoning him up to whine away about her.

It also explained something else. Mrs Bent had said to Elizabeth 'You signed the letters you wrote, you weren't anonymous'. Mrs Bent was saying that nothing written in them was true, it was even malicious, so of course she might think Elizabeth would want no one to know who she was.

Another witness whom Mrs Bent ignored later wrote to the director: 'I realise that to a relative stranger Elizabeth's explanation of events may sound fragmented and a little far fetched, but I can categorically assure you that what she's saying is true.' She didn't know it shouldn't have sounded far fetched to Mrs Bent. It should have sounded like a routine case. If Elizabeth and her mother had been living in a different town with completely different social workers there is very little doubt that they would have taken their side and sorted it all out in days.

In Elizabeth's case, apart from everything else, if she had been as deranged as they were making out she would have been showing other symptoms. She certainly wouldn't have been able to go out every day doing charity work. All this reflected in something the psychiatrist said. 'As soon as I saw you walking down the street, I thought, she doesn't think she's God.' Yet Mrs Bent had told him that Elizabeth was calling herself God. He had been expecting to see a raving lunatic.

He had also expressed surprise at a remark Mrs Bent had made to him about Elizabeth not getting home from work until after five o'clock. 'From work?' he had exclaimed, knowing that people who think they're God are not likely to go to work. 'Oh yes' she had replied, 'She's out of the house every morning before nine and sometimes doesn't get in until after six.'

Much later, it seemed, Elizabeth discovered that Mrs Bent hadn't dismissed everything as delusional. She wrote without excusing him in any way, 'I have seen an abusive letter Paul Stalker sent to Elizabeth.' Yet some people still wonder. It was on a page they had taken out to start off with, because it had something confidential on it about someone else. When Elizabeth saw it later she thought how typically careless it had been of them to let her see it. Now she didn't think so. With all the corruption she'd been faced with since, she wondered if they had decided to let her see it after all and to spice it up a bit.

When Elizabeth first saw the mess her notes were in, she knew she would never get Social Services to correct them. She was vulnerable, small and weak, they were big and powerful. She knew it was common practice among them to resist strongly any criticism or complaints; it was a formidable task asking them to put anything right. Although she found it all very stressful, she had nevertheless been expecting it. She already knew that if a social worker writes a report with everything wrong in it, it is the patient who is blamed and treated as a nuisance when she tries to get them to correct it, not the social worker who got it wrong in the first place. It was all so frustrating - the mistakes were so easily provable. It could all have been put right in a couple of days and then she could have forgotten about it all and put it all behind her. But she knew she had no chance of that and another nightmare was about to begin.

She was well aware that she might not be able to live in her own home any more, that they would treat her complaint as a mental health problem and harass her. She was very concerned about her cat, Poppy. Who would look after her if they had to go? Would they be able to take her with them? She was a very old cat; they had loved her for fifteen years. She still enjoyed life, but she was a bad traveller.

One time when they had to flee they left Poppy in the hands of a man who was staying in the house with them, who promised them he would look after her. He never had any intention of doing so; he just wanted to get them out of the place so that he could have it to himself. As soon as they had gone he chucked the cat out. They never found out what happened to her. They never forgave Social Services for that. They had been told that they were creating very big problems with the cat, yet neither Elizabeth nor her mother imagined anything like this would happen. It wasn't just any cat, it was Poppy, their cat. Elizabeth didn't realise what a close bond she had had with her until she was gone. And of course, there was no proper closure. They weren't there to say goodbye to the cat, and they weren't there to give her comfort when she was dying, or to see to it that she died a painless death. It was something that would haunt Elizabeth for years to come.

Chapter Six

RED TAPE

If there had been regulations to cover it, it might have been possible to get Mrs Bent's mental health assessed in a couple of days. Later, three psychologists, all independent of one another, gave the same opinion. To them it was a very typical case. Many people have said since that if a patient has good reason to think there's something wrong with a health official, there should be a way they can get that person checked. No chance - the ministers are too much in denial. In a suggestion for the new Mental Health Act (2007) put forward by the ministers, it said, 'anyone can put in a request for someone to have their mental health assessed; all reasonable requests should be granted.' Who decides what's reasonable? The ministers also made mention of malicious requests, but who decides what's reasonable and what's malicious? In this case, it was Mrs Bent.

If Elizabeth had known what a fight the authorities would put up and how very unscrupulous and ruthless they would be, she wouldn't have started it. She would have left the notes as they were and hoped that as they faded into history no one would see them. She would never advise anyone to try to get notes corrected, or at least, to make certain they knew what they were taking on. Some other solution would have to be found.

It also worried her how much of this was deliberate. Was it careless, reckless or calculated? Her notes were full of what she had told and told Mrs Bent NOT to say. 'Don't say I said Paul Stalker has murdered a woman, make it clear that I only said he told me he has' - yet she still wrote the former in the report. It was as though it gave her a buzz to show Elizabeth she had to accept what she said.

It's like a man who drives a car through a red traffic light at 60 miles an hour. It isn't because he's in a hurry – he does know how to drive safely - it's a message of defiance.

Some of the mistakes didn't matter much - for example, she said she had aunts when she had none - but some were more serious. The problem was that either way Elizabeth was risking her health. While trying to get it corrected she was getting ulcers on the face and in the mouth, seeing bright lights associated with constriction of the arteries to the eyes and suffered migraine headaches, plus other symptoms that the Coronary Prevention Group say need avoiding. But not getting notes corrected was another health hazard. A doctor going by the wrong history might make the wrong diagnosis and give the wrong treatment.

Mrs Bent said there was old and dirty food lying about the house. Not true. Elizabeth was well aware this would be encouraging vermin.

It took them three years to correct her notes to show that she had never been admitted into hospital under a section of the Mental Health Act. The problem was that by denying it and persevering with trying to get it put right, Elizabeth was drawing attention to it and making it worse. People who had never thought about it before now began to wonder. It's all very well saying you shouldn't talk about it, but you can be so upset about a thing that you have to.

Elizabeth didn't even like people knowing she had a psychiatric history; she had suffered so much discrimination. At the time when Mrs Bent first appointed herself as her social worker, Elizabeth had no trouble keeping that a secret. She had been better for such a long time that it was no longer a part of her life. She never talked or thought about it. People just assumed she'd always been sane.

Unfortunately, her denying this compulsory admission into hospital was also creating another problem. It was suggesting it was something shameful. She was afraid of offending people who had been, or their relatives. She had to make it clear what her point was, that a wrong history could finish up with the wrong treatment being administrated.

Those who had known her a long time and knew she had never been admitted started saying "It's best to leave it there and hope that as it fades into history no one sees it." And as time went by, Elizabeth realized they were right. For one thing, they could see it was making her ill.

One very well-meaning remark she got was, "I don't care what you've done in the past." They were wondering what dark history she had to hide. She was also asked, 'Are you sure you never have been? I mean, you didn't think you were going in voluntarily when you were under a section?' They would give her assurances at the same time that we all make mistakes.

They were not only preparing her for the shock of finding out she had been, but did not want her to feel very silly. It was they who got the shock, not Elizabeth. They looked very shocked when it came out that it was the social worker's mistake, not Elizabeth's. Mrs Bent said that she had concluded this after talking to a psychiatrist. Elizabeth did know what the psychiatrist had actually said. He could find no record of it, so Mrs Bent would not have it. She merely stated "Date and circumstances unknown." It was going according to Paul Stalker too. She refused to accept it that Elizabeth never had been. Even after this she did not accept the doctor's statement to the solicitor: 'I can confirm there's never been a compulsory admission into hospital.' False beliefs can be very fixed, and it can be a nightmare getting notes changed when they're wrong.

The nightmares returned. She didn't know which was worse, the nightmares or the insomnia. She was afraid to nod off for a second for fear of what she might dream. She kept having the same two dreams. In one she was struggling in water, about to go under, about to drown, and in the other she was helplessly watching someone else drown. She saw a bus go into the lake and slowly sink, and there was nothing she could do for the people in it. She felt it was some sort of a message to her - 'You're clutching at straws, no matter how many people you're trying to save you won't succeed.' She realised when she woke up that it was largely the principle she was fighting for. She wanted to make it possible for a patient to be able to complain.

When Elizabeth complained about Mrs Bent's repeated statement on what was libel, the authorities wrote and told her, 'There was a difference in interpretation in what was said between you and Mrs Bent with no corroborating evidence to support either view.' But there was evidence. It was very clear what she wrote in the report. If they had looked at that they would have seen very firm evidence. But they didn't believe in checking up.

The solicitor had seen Mrs Bent's comments about libel in the notes and wrote to tell Social Services to put it right. They wrote back and told him he was welcome to his opinion, which they called 'your client's views', next to Mrs Bent's statement. Yet lawyer after lawyer had told Elizabeth that judges decide what is libel and certainly not social workers.

It is another typical case of Social Services not knowing the difference between opinion and fact. The solicitor didn't give any views on it, he gave confirmation that it was not libel. It was as though a doctor had seen a statement in a solicitor's letter that a patient of his had had his appendix out when this was not the case and he had written to tell them to correct it, and been told he was welcome to his opinion on the matter. The fact this was not libel was just as clear cut.

The director also said in a letter how hard several social workers had tried to help Elizabeth. He failed to mention at the same time that this help had not been the kind she had requested. It was psychiatric and social assistance they had been trying to give her, whereas the help she had asked for was to correct her notes and answer her questions.

The director then said how very difficult Elizabeth was and that he did not know how to deal with such a person. In response to that four people all wrote in separately to tell him how to deal with her - he should correct her notes, answer her questions and look into her new complaint about a lie which Mrs Bent had told.

It was quite worrying that Social Services seemed to be so deluded. They seemed to believe that Mrs Bent hadn't done anything wrong, that the only help Elizabeth needed was psychiatric and social. Despite the fact that they were all so dedicated and so patient, they had failed to give her this help. And they had failed because Elizabeth was such a 'difficult person'.

Were they really as deluded as that? Did they really believe that their only interest was in the health and welfare of Elizabeth? Did they imagine that the public wouldn't be able to see what their motive was? They were opening themselves up to ridicule if so. Yet it seemed so. The director sounded quite frustrated that he couldn't 'take care' of Elizabeth.

They had lost the fight to persuade her to accept their 'help' or to be able to speak to her face to face so that they could make things up about her. They had lost the fight to be able to use force. They had tried without success to put her into a mental hospital.

At least the doctors refused to be a party to it. None of them tried in any way to get Elizabeth to believe that anything that Mrs Bent had said was reasonable or sensible or that she had any good intentions.

In a letter to her MP, Social Services talked as though it was not normal behaviour for someone to complain about them. This was before they had even begun to correct any of the mistakes in her notes. In fact it was in the same year that two letters from a solicitor, both about the alleged compulsory admission into hospital, were lost. The Director talked as though they were fully supported by a psychiatrist, but they were not. The director said 'A further assessment under the Mental Health Act does seem indicated, particularly as the letter writing and complaints about Mrs Bent could be construed as a symptom of her deteriorating mental health.' It was like Russia under communism – complaining is not considered normal behaviour. They were putting people who opposed the government into mental hospitals.

Elizabeth believed that if Paul Stalker had sued her and lost the case, Mrs Bent would have seen it as a miscarriage of justice. Even a court could not have convinced her. She might even have pretended that somehow Stalker had won. False beliefs can be very fixed.

The Social Services Director got several things wrong in letters. He mistook which neighbours the solicitor was talking about, a mistake which could cause trouble. He also made mistakes at various times with Elizabeth's first name, her address and her previous address, which meant her mother's address was wrong too as next of kin. Elizabeth was most anxious that they should put that right as it was crucial that the right relative should be contacted in a crisis, but it was never corrected. They were determined to keep it wrong for the same reason that Elizabeth was so keen to put it right; it would suit them to use Sisley as next of kin by 'mistake'. She'd go along with anything they said.

Elizabeth believed that the house Mrs Bent had said they were living in had been blown up during the war, when the Germans were trying to bomb the railway lines. Yet she had worked in offices, so she knew how some of these mistakes can be made, such as through a typist not being able to read a secretary's shorthand properly. And she doubted Mrs Bent would look at what she was signing.

In fact it took Elizabeth back a while to when she had once

mistyped 'farmyards' and the man who had dictated the letter had said nothing about it. It was later brought up at a meeting about the clerks not having a clue as to what it was they were typing, but in that office they had a much higher standard than Social Services for what they called 'very efficient'.

They told the Elders that Mrs Bent worked with 'thoroughness'. A remark like that is asking for sarcasm. People are going to ask, 'thoroughness about what?' That was after they had put in 15 complaints about her - none of which were upheld.

* * * * * * * *

Later in her notes, Mrs Bent was talking again about getting control over the lives of Elizabeth and her mother. She wrote how they both might gain from social intervention and how Mrs Elders might benefit from having someone to help her with personal needs, self-help tasks, shopping, laundry and cooking. She must have calculated that to start up again like that, to start interfering again, would once more drive Elizabeth mad and might even get her screaming on the floor like a madwoman. In fact, in the same notes, only a couple of pages earlier, she had written, 'Elizabeth is very resistant to intervention'. Yet now she was planning on intervening again, going into which doctor and social worker to involve. The doctor was the one who said he'd do his best to get rid of her for her, the social worker was the one who had been there when Elizabeth had been shouting at her in the street 'Go away and never come back again!' If she tried it, she failed – neither of them came.

When Elizabeth had just come out of hospital after having had two major operations, a home help called Mrs Turner went to the house to see her. According to Mrs Bent she was talking about Elizabeth as though she was completely deranged. She got her facts quite wrong. This issue has been voiced in the House of Lords, when they were discussing what powers to give to social workers should their interest be to help the patient. One of the Lords stood up and said, 'That's wide open to abuse, how do we know they haven't invented the lot of it?'

When Elizabeth said she'd received two short calls in two weeks in which no one spoke, Mrs Bent remained sceptical despite Stalker being a notorious telephone nutter. She was prepared to treat it as a 'psychotic episode' (her words) and talked about taking over her life for her. But far more amazing was that Mrs Turner apparently said that Elizabeth had claimed that Paul Stalker had been locked up and had somehow escaped. Elizabeth's comment at the time was 'If she really did say all that about me, I can only say she's as barmy as Mrs Bent'.

* * * * * * * *

The authorities sent Elizabeth a four-page letter explaining how they could do whatever they liked, whether she wanted them to or not. They could bully her endlessly. The system was wide open to abuse and was in urgent need of being reformed. Her solicitor said she should contact the Government about it, so she wrote to them all, the House of Commons, the House of Lords, but when it got back to Social Services that she had written to her MP they asked a psychiatrist to section her, inventing information to make their case. The psychiatrist wrote in a letter back to them: 'It would be helpful if I could see a copy of the MP's letter so that I can have a better idea of the concern you are addressing, and in particular whether or not there is a need to reassess her as suitable for detention under the Mental Health Act.'

Elizabeth and her mother wanted it putting into the Act that the patient has the right to insist the psychiatrist sees the letter they are acting upon, and not be allowed to please himself.

The MP made a big mistake in contacting Social Services to let them know Elizabeth had written to him about them. It was a mistake she had to pay for very heavily. She had told him that she wanted an easy, straightforward way for notes to be corrected and she thought that if she gave herself as an example he would see what she meant. She never expected him to contact them about it and he never expected them to treat it as a mental health problem. He expected them to correct her notes.

When Elizabeth first put in her complaints she discovered something else very worrying; both Mrs Bent and her team leader had told a very serious lie. They both told the Complaints Officer that they had never said anything to Elizabeth to imply that she would be sectioned. It may sound silly to put in another complaint when they had already driven her to the brink of a nervous breakdown, but this was a very serious lie. They were saying that it was Elizabeth and her mother who had caused the big panic when Elizabeth had to be rushed into hiding. It was going to make people think they were both paranoid.

Mrs Bent had no remorse for what she had done. She didn't try to make it into a smaller lie, to say something like 'It seems I didn't make myself clear and was misinterpreted' - she just kept on telling the same lies. She didn't care how much damage it could do to Elizabeth or how much embarrassment it would cause to her colleagues when she got them involved.

The authorities continued to treat Mrs Bent as though she was sensible and reliable. The director wrote in a letter, 'Mrs Bent found that it was very difficult to receive any co-operation from Elizabeth, due to her conviction that social workers wanted to section her.'

Elizabeth, after finding it impossible to write herself to protest that she was vulnerable, managed to get someone else to do it for her, someone with no psychiatric history. They said: *'This is very much implying that social workers hadn't wanted to section her and that it was paranoia for her to think so. Yet according to her solicitor her own doctor told him they had asked him to do this. It cannot be considered paranoia to believe the words of one's own solicitor or doctor. The truth is that social workers are capable of telling lies and then using the patient's complaint about it as evidence that they are mentally ill.'*

They are not the only ones. Firstly Sisley's husband was violent with her and then claimed that her reporting it was evidence that she was unstable. Secondly, Paul Stalker was telling her he'd murdered a woman, so that he could undermine her when she repeated it.

Now back to the man who wrote in on Elizabeth's behalf. He said *'It appears this tissue of lies is being used to harass her in her own home. Despite the fact that social workers concerned were fully aware she had forbidden them to visit and that she would be very upset by their call, their reply to her saying, 'You can't come round here' was nevertheless, 'yes we can.' This can only be construed as an attempt to traumatise, to induce something like the paranoia previously ascribed to her.'*

As regards sending the other social workers round to the house, knowing how much it had upset her, the director wrote in a letter: *'Two of them went on the advice of Mrs Bent who said that, in view of Elizabeth's tendency to make accusations against social workers, it would be wise to have a witness present.'* They took advice from the one she was complaining about on what to do about it.

This is another example of the pot calling the kettle black, indeed there needed to be a witness present should Mrs Bent be in the house. But there is a much more important point. Someone wrote in on Elizabeth's behalf about it: *'This was said as though such allegations were false. In fact, nothing Elizabeth has said turned out to be untrue, although the department has declined to investigate a lot of the criticisms she has made. It's a great shame that when Mrs Bent was giving advice about these unwanted visits she didn't say, 'Don't go, she's forbidden it, she'll be very upset' or better still, 'She's right, I did tell a lie'. I fully appreciate that to admit to something like that is difficult, but Mrs Bent seems to have gone out of her way to show she had neither conscious nor remorse. It is also a great pity that instead of trying to assess Elizabeth's mental health, they didn't do as she requested, correct her notes, answer her questions and look into this one further complaint she has made - this lie that Mrs Bent has told.'*

When it first started Elizabeth tried to get hold of another social worker who could be a witness that Mrs Bent had told this lie, but he had left. So she wrote asking where he was, explaining why she wanted to know. But this was treated as a mental health problem and they sent round another social worker, who we'll call Mrs Maffee - social workers have been called the 'do-gooders' mafia'.

Unfortunately Mrs Maffee was another one who didn't mind telling lies, another who was thoroughly corrupt. Someone wrote in on Elizabeth's behalf and said: *'It has been noticed in answer to her question 'Where is Mr X now?' she has been told 'We can't help you there, we'll send round another social worker who can help you instead'. This strikes us as strange. Elizabeth's letter seems clear on what help she needs. She wants a witness. Mr X would know it was a lie that Mrs Bent has told. So how can she help her? She wasn't there at the time. We can see though how she can help Mrs Bent. She can visit Elizabeth, make up information about her, stop this complaint about her being investigated and get it treated as a mental health problem instead.'*

They said they couldn't cope with the volume of letters Elizabeth wrote. These were graduates in psychiatry, trained to manage the maddest of the mad, and it was only an average of one 300-word letter every two weeks. The Mental Health Advocacy very quickly summed it all up in less than 500 words, and the MP took even less to sum up the bits which concerned him. Some of the material was just photocopies of the same thing, reminders that Elizabeth kept sending in. Some of the letters had fewer than twenty words in them and were arranged so that they could be answered yes or no. They'd manage over 6000 words to defend themselves.

Elizabeth put in one further complaint as soon as she heard about it, but they denied having received it even though they had answered it. The left hand did not know what the right hand was doing. They said it was a complaint which had already been investigated and they wouldn't look into the same complaint twice. In fact they hadn't looked into it once.

It upset Elizabeth very much that they kept saying she had put in a complaint that had already been investigated. She found it insulting. Eventually a solicitor wrote in on her behalf to ask to see what records they had to prove such a claim. They didn't answer, but they did stop making the claim.

Elizabeth was in their office when they told her they had received her complaint too late. She went home and was violently sick. She felt ill for two days and wondered if she had caught a bug - stress takes down the resistance. She had persevered for so long, sent in the complaint in plenty of time and kept sending in reminders for so long, and all she had got from it was more harassment, more unwanted visits from Social Services, more lies. But when she complained about the lies they said they had looked into these complaints too. She saw where they had written 'A thorough and formal investigation into these allegations concerning Mrs Bent and Mrs Maffee has already been carried out, in 1996. These complaints were not upheld. The findings were conveyed to Elizabeth at the time.'

In fact nothing was conveyed to Elizabeth. The only way they could have had a record of this investigation is by downright fraud.

Eventually they admitted that they had received it but hadn't looked into it. They blamed Elizabeth for this. They made her out to be a very awkward person. She saw written in a letter in her notes,

'*There is clear evidence of strenuous attempts to engage Elizabeth in such a process*'. Elizabeth wrote in and asked to see the details of these 'strenuous attempts' and they sent her copies of papers showing how they had tried to help her with psychiatric and social care.

The evidence they had to say Mrs Bent had said nothing to suggest Elizabeth would be sectioned was first that Mrs Bent had denied it, and second that an important document was never prepared. This document was a special report that a social worker has to write if someone is to be sectioned. The authorities say there was no document because Mrs Bent was never planning to section her. With Mrs Bent being so reckless and the authorities so corrupt, there is no knowing if it ever existed or if they destroyed it.

They also refused to ask her own doctor, despite a solicitor's request. Yet they used the fact that another doctor had made no mention of the plan in a written report to section Elizabeth as evidence that there was no such plan.

They held a meeting about the case, referring to 'slanderous material'. The solicitor had seen the mistakes in the report, which showed that they did not know the difference between slander (defamatory statements made verbally) and libel (when they are made in writing). On top of all this, social workers didn't seem to know the difference between criminal and civil law, or even what common law was, nor had they bothered to find out – perhaps because they did not want to.

Elizabeth continued to worry that the doctors were afraid of being sued. They would especially fear this with a family that had money.

Elizabeth and her mother had promised themselves not to let any social workers inside the house, and to put everything said to them in writing. Keeping them out had been like keeping a dog out of the house when you have a bitch on heat, and they continued to fabricate what Elizabeth had said. There was, and is, nothing in the Mental Health Act to say they have to look at letters.

They were determined to get into the house for the same reason Elizabeth and her mother were determined to keep them out. Both sides knew they could get far more power by seeing people face to face, and it is much easier to make up what the patient has said or done.

The social workers were clearly told by Elizabeth and her mother not to come to the house any more, but Social Services made it equally clear that they were determined to keep on visiting. They knew they were causing chaos. Elizabeth suspected it gave them a buzz to use their power like this.

When Elizabeth and her mother were driven out of the back door into the pouring rain, two social workers pretended to look compassionately on. No one was taken in. At least one neighbour looking out of the window had said once before, 'Those social workers don't half need a kick up the backside'. A director wrote 'Mrs Maffee didn't think it would be appropriate to apprehend them in the street.' Since the Prevention of Harassment Act 1997, it would be appropriate for the police to apprehend them. They could warn them or even caution them.

Mrs Maffee did try to get social workers in Kent, where Elizabeth had sought sanctuary, to be a party to it, but they immediately smelled a rat, and their suspicions were confirmed by a solicitor. All they would say to Elizabeth and her mother was, 'As long as you know where we are if you need us.' It was a dreadful shame that they couldn't go home, but it was impossible. In 1994 one of Elizabeth's complaints had been that neither Mrs Bent nor the team leader responded to a request for written assurances that they wouldn't return to the house. The answer they got was: *'Under The Mental Health Act 1983, no social worker can give such an assurance when statutory duties may require such a visit.'*

As soon as Elizabeth wanted notes correcting and questions answering, they considered that statutory duties did require such a visit. It's a dangerous game to ask too many questions.

One visitor who stayed in the house for a short while was a woman called Madeleine, who had a long psychiatric history and had once been diagnosed with schizophrenia. In Madeleine's case this simply meant that she was unusually quiet and withdrawn. She was in the care of the mental health team in a different area, and had never had any complaints about them. Yet social workers in Elizabeth's area used her as an excuse to harass Elizabeth. In a letter to the local MP, the director said she had schizophrenia, giving her name and that of her psychiatrist. He named the wrong psychiatrist and the wrong department. Knowing that Madeleine had seen what was going on at the Elder's home, the director wanted to ensure she had no say.

She also wanted to give the MP the impression that the house was dangerous and that it was necessary for her get inside. That's the trouble with being labelled; you are open to blackmail, and it won't necessarily be you who is the victim. Someone like Madeleine could blame Elizabeth if confidential details about her got out. It could break up a friendship.

As Social Services knew who Madeleine's doctor was, Elizabeth suspected that they had made this mistake on purpose. They didn't want the right one brought in for fear of it being shown up that they couldn't get any support from him.

Madeleine was very upset that the MP was told all this about her. Yet the director is bound to put up the defence that breach of confidentiality was necessary to protect Mrs Elders. They said repeatedly that she could be at risk, particularly when they found out how often Madeleine was in the house.

Madeleine felt that was libel. She said she had never been a threat to anyone, and so did other people who had known her a long time, including her mother. It could hardly be libel to call someone a schizophrenic if a psychiatrist had diagnosed them as such. But if something was being said to deliberately mislead, to get actions and opinions based on inaccurate information, the position was less clear. Would the MP know what a schizophrenic was? Could it be called defamation of character to say someone was schizophrenic?

Since they were making the claim that their concern here was for Mrs Elders, Elizabeth wanted to know why they didn't contact her mother's own doctor about it. As they were saying Madeleine could be a threat to her, why didn't they also contact Madeleine's doctor? They wanted to keep to their original, false evidence. They wanted to maintain opinions based on guesswork. They continued to use Madeleine as an excuse, then they used her to pass on made-up information about Elizabeth to someone else. They were clutching at straws, scraping the bottom of the barrel. Their plans were failing.

* * * * * * * *

Mrs Bent went out for a stroll one evening, feeling thoroughly depressed. When it began to rain she sought shelter in a pub. It was only seven o'clock and the place was almost empty. She decided to go inside and have a snack. There were some sandwiches on the bar and she bought one with an orange juice. As she sat there quietly another woman, aged about 25, slim and beautiful with blond hair, spoke to her. She introduced herself as Sally Wilkinson. When Sally told her that she too was a social worker, she began to pour her heart out. Sally listened sympathetically.

'It's a pity we can't get her to do something really mad' said Sally, 'something to get people to sit up, something to make the doctors agree she does come under the Mental Health Act. Maybe you could get her to send the story about you to someone who will be really upset, so we can call it malicious?'

'Good idea' said Mrs Bent. She had thought about this before. She bought Sally another drink.

'I'll phone Elizabeth up' said Sally. 'I'll say I've heard about the book she's writing, I'll say I'd love to have a copy of it.'

They headed for a phone box, giggling together. Sally telephoned Elizabeth, asking her to send a copy of the manuscript of the book and giving her address. It went perfectly to plan. Elizabeth was completely taken in. She posted her a copy to Sally the next morning, and the following day Sally phoned Mrs Bent to tell her it had arrived.

'Oh please complain about it!' said Mrs Bent.

'I will, I will' said Sally, equally enthusiastic 'Will you meet me tonight?'

They met up that evening. Sally clearly drank a lot, but Mrs Bent was very willing to buy her a few more drinks. It was worth it.

'You will phone up and complain?' she earnestly asked her again.

'I'll do it now' said Sally, and again they went into the phone box together. Mrs Bent was amazed at how well she could act. Sally said the book had come as a complete surprise to her, deliberately omitting to say that she had requested it. She complained that it was about something particularly upsetting.

'Brilliant, brilliant' said Mrs Bent and they both went giggling back into the pub. They finished off their drinks and then went into an off licence, where Mrs Bent bought a bottle of whisky for Sally to take home with her.

'I might call on you to help me again' she said.

'Any time' Sally replied.

The police interviewed Sally about it and then went round to see Elizabeth. They merely told her not to send anything else. Elizabeth said she'd been the victim of a hoax phone call. The police seemed willing to believe that, and said they weren't going to take it any further.

Elizabeth suspected that Mrs Bent had something to do with it, so she telephoned the department where she worked in Grimley. Mr

Baker, who was head of the department, had only started that day. He spoke to Mrs Bent about it. He was completely unaware of how very strange she could be. She told him, 'Oh that's very typical of Elizabeth. I tried so hard to help her.' Then she went on to tell him she thought it would be wise to inform the Mental Health Team in Gorsedale, where Elizabeth was now living. 'Let them know that she's in their jurisdiction, find out if they're giving her the help she needs' she said.

Mr Baker wasn't going to do it just like that; he felt he needed to telephone the police first to find out precisely what had happened. Mrs Bent hoped the police would tell him that Elizabeth had done something really mad and that she was malicious. After Mr Baker had finished speaking to them she took the notes that he had written on it, went through them with him and said, 'Leave it to me.' She passed it on to another social worker who hadn't been working there long either, who wasn't as well qualified as she was, and told her to phone up Social Services in Gorsedale. But before she handed the notes over she made substantial changes to them.

However, this plan backfired. The same thing happened in Gorsedale as had happened in Kent. The social workers immediately smelled a rat. If the police were so worried about Elizabeth's mental health, why hadn't they contacted them about her? Why were they saying all these things to social workers in a different area who had nothing to do with the case? It especially surprised them as it is quite a serious thing to say that someone is mentally ill. How could they be so careless as to say so much to someone whom it didn't concern?

It crossed their mind that the police hadn't really said all these things at all. Maybe someone had made it all up - someone who had a grudge against Elizabeth? A social worker who Elizabeth had complained about, perhaps.

Some of these suspicions were confirmed by a solicitor. The

Gorsedale team did go round to see Elizabeth about it, but they told her they wouldn't begin to consider taking any action over it until the police contacted them, if at all. They assured her they would leave her alone. They didn't even want to know who her own doctor was. As far as they were concerned, Elizabeth didn't exist. 'As long as you know where we are if you need us' they said.

They told her what Social Services in Grimley had told them the police had said – that a funny smell was coming from the house and they suspected Elizabeth had someone elderly in there and was neglecting them. If that were true, even if only suspected, it would give them a lot of power. It would mean they could force their way inside the house. But the Grimley report had said the police officer hadn't stopped at that. He had said that Elizabeth was only willing to speak to him through a little crack in the door. It was indeed an example of what William Blake said: 'A truth told with bad intent can beat all the lies that hell can invent.'

It was deliberately misleading, and had clearly been designed to make Elizabeth sound paranoid. Mrs Bent had greatly altered the notes. She had made certain there was no mention that Elizabeth had a dog that was trying to get out, and she had crossed out the bit which said that Elizabeth had invited him into the house.

Yet the real bombshell was the statement 'She has a history of complaining'. They did not say that she had only ever complained about them.

When Elizabeth looked into it, she could find no social worker with the name of Sally Wilkinson, and certainly not in the department where she had said she worked. This confirmed that 'Sally' was a complete fraud.

Chapter Seven

SANITY AND DELUSIONS

Things started getting on top of Mrs Bent again. She wasn't used to failing to get control, and most certainly she had never met anything like this. She began to wish she had never started it.

Her niece had been to see her again and left the house spotless. It was nice to see it so clean, and now she was alone again, as she liked it. She went upstairs to bed early that night and tried not to worry, but once she was fast asleep the nightmares started coming back. This time she was being taken away in a yellow van, but she didn't know where to except that it was out in the country. Maybe she was going to prison - or maybe they were going to put her in a mental hospital. Were they saying she had committed a crime, or that she was mad? Everything was in a terrible muddle. Then the van started going round a corner, trees were on either side hitting against the window, and she cried out 'Wrong way, we're going the wrong way!'

But no one was taking any notice.

When she awoke she thought there was someone else in the room. It was pitch black, yet she could sense it. She called out 'Is that you?' but there was no answer. She got out of bed and felt her way out on to the landing to put the light on. She couldn't see anyone. She looked in all the rooms upstairs. No one was there. Then she went downstairs and had a good look all round there too, but couldn't find anyone.

She realised it had all been part of the dream, and that she was alone. She made herself some coffee and drew the curtains open so that she could see anyone going by. That somehow made her feel safe. By now it was midnight and she knew she must get back to bed and sleep, for she had to get up early next morning.

But she was no sooner asleep than she began to dream again. She was still in the same yellow van going along the road, only this time it stopped. The driver got out and went away and she seized the opportunity to escape. She found the door unlocked, so she jumped out. She was free.

That was good, but where could she escape to? She had no idea where she was as she walked down a lonely road with a hedge on both sides. Daylight was coming, and now a tractor came along, pulling a cart behind it. It couldn't have come at a better moment for she also saw a prison guard approaching, a young, slim woman with short blonde hair, in a navy blue uniform. Mrs Bent immediately jumped on the cart. The prison officer spotted her and began to run towards her and chase the tractor. She got so very close, how fast she could run! Mrs Bent could very clearly see her knees with her navy blue skirt just above it as she raced along. Yet every time she got that little bit closer, almost close enough to jump on and get Mrs Bent, the tractor drove that little bit faster. The driver was completely unaware of what was going on behind him.

Eventually the prison officer fell further and further behind. Mrs Bent was free again. She lay down and relaxed in the hay. The prison officer was now out of sight.

When she awoke there was a ginger cat on the window sill, crying to get in. She wondered if this was what she'd heard the night before that had made her think there was someone else in the house. The dream she had had gave her great peace of mind. Some of these people might seem tough, but she would always beat them.

She had had such dreams before. In one of them she'd been climbing out of the window of a very big and old-fashioned Victorian building. She was squeezing between bars, got on to a roof, and then looked down at all the freedom beneath her. 'How am I going to get down there?' She wondered. Then she thought she could hear people beneath her. Were they climbing up a drainpipe - coming up to get her? Maybe they were on a ladder. Then an alarm went off and they knew she was out. The prison was alive with activity.

She rolled over in bed to turn off her alarm clock, realising it was just another dream. 'They can't catch up with me' she thought. 'I will always escape.' She went to work that morning feeling very smug. She felt it wouldn't be long before Elizabeth was defeated.

* * * * * * * *

If it is found that a man is in prison or a mental hospital for something he didn't do, they let him out. But in the case of forced adoptions, regardless of how innocent the parents are later found to be, it's too late. Their children have gone. They never see them again.

It's been said that the police will have a man in prison for a crime he didn't commit rather than admit that they had the wrong man. It seems Social Services would rather have had Elizabeth in a mental hospital than admit that a social worker had done anything wrong. This reminded Elizabeth of another example of how 'uniforms stick together'. Who remembers the Polish man who serve 15 years for killing a child? No one could have been more innocent than he was. That crime had nothing to do with him, yet the prison psychiatrist wrote in the notes 'He has delusions of innocence.' He wasn't going to consider for a second that another uniform could make such a mistake, but the evidence they had to convict him was circumstantial. However hard the man tried to argue that he was innocent, the psychiatrist wasn't going to see it. It was the psychiatrist who had delusions – delusions of someone else's guilt.

In mental hospitals they can retreat with grace. They can say, 'Look at how sane this man is! Doesn't it show how effective our treatment is?' They have no need to mention that there was nothing wrong with him in the first place.

Take the murders at 10 Rillington Place in the 1950s. After they executed Timothy Evans for the murder of his wife and child, more bodies started turning up. People began to ask questions. It looked more and more as though they had hanged the wrong man. When John Christie was under sentence of death for the murders of six women in the same house, there were calls for the hanging to be delayed because the public did not want Christie to take the true story of what had happened in that house with him to his grave. They wanted the authorities to make sure the same mistake would not be made again. Yet the authorities rushed to execute him despite the public outcry, because they wanted to cover up their bungling.

Elizabeth knew she shouldn't compare such a horrendous case with the trouble she had had with Social Services, yet it may be only the extreme cases that reach the public eye. She was most sceptical about encouraging a patient to complain. It hadn't been safe for her to do so.

Social Services would have had Elizabeth in a mental hospital rather than put the report right. They would also have said her mother wasn't being looked after properly, and put her into a home. The things that could have happened don't bear thinking about. She believed it was wrong for any member of staff to explain the complaints procedure to anyone who is vulnerable, or at least to lead them to believe they are perfectly free to complain. Once they have succeeded in driving a patient into a nervous breakdown they will have more power than ever.

Elizabeth knew of a case where a patient had alleged that a doctor had punched him in the stomach. The other doctors were very keen that the allegation should be investigated. Of course they were - they knew beforehand what the outcome would be - his name had to be cleared. She wanted the same rights for the patients - if wild allegations were made against them, they too should have them looked into.

* * * * * * * *

Elizabeth again became a victim of 'looping', where anything you say to defend yourself is turned round and used against you. A solicitor told her that what they had written about her wasn't libel, as it hadn't done her any damage. So she told her doctor not to act upon anything they said. Next she went to see the local psychiatrist - not as a patient but to tell him the same thing and explain that her notes were all wrong.

She made a big mistake there. She should have asked her solicitor to phone him up and tell him. When it got back to Social Services that she'd been to see the psychiatrist they started calling him 'her psychiatrist' and talked as though she was being treated on a regular basis. He responded to what they told him about her by making more appointments to see her – which she did not know about, because she had been driven out of her house and was not getting her post. They were then able to accuse her of not keeping her appointments.

When she later talked to him about the whole thing, he said that the honest truth was that he couldn't remember a lot of it. Yet there was one thing he did clearly remember. He wanted to emphasise that not for a second would he consider having her sectioned, seemingly having forgotten something he'd written in a letter. Elizabeth had seen it. She didn't point it out to him or start to argue. She assumed he was going entirely by what Social Services were telling him. She believed it was like a driving examiner who will consider passing anyone until he seems them drive.

She saw that he had written in a letter to them: '*The views that you attribute to me are incorrect. I would be grateful if in future you consulted me before quoting my opinion to her MP or any other official.*'

The other example of looping she suffered was when they asked her whether she would mind them seeing what another doctor had said about her. She didn't mind at all. She'd read her notes and knew what he'd put. In fact, not to allow it might arouse suspicion. It would suggest she had something to hide.

She was in for another shock. They had managed to interpret everything he had said as agreeing with Mrs Bent. Elizabeth wrote the following letter to them about it.

Dear Social Services,

As regards you saying a psychiatrist wrote a report on me consistent with Mrs Bent's report, please could you send me a list of the same mistakes he made and a list of the same delusions he said I was having and a copy of his statement that what I had written was libel when that's for a lawyer to say, ultimately a judge and most certainly not a doctor. Could you please also send me a copy of his bad grammar with inverted commas missing so no one can tell who said what. The punctuation makes it look as if the police and the neighbours confirmed for her what was libel, and not Paul Stalker, a notorious liar.

Could you please, when you mention, 'equivocal delusions', make it clear who it was that was questioning it. He meant Mrs Bent, Paul Stalker and

Sisley, although he got that bit wrong. They weren't questioning it. They confirmed it. They made a statement. They said, 'Elizabeth is deluded.'

Could you also please, when you say he shared his concern about her mental health, make it clear his concerns were for a completely different reason. Mrs Bent was talking about libel. He never mentioned it once. His concern was that I was being harassed, driven into a nervous breakdown and possibly to suicide. He only came out to see me because she was saying all this about me and he would go out to see anyone after hearing all that.

As regards bad punctuation, of course we didn't see any of the scribbled-out notes she gave to the clerk to type out.

Throughout it all they seemed to think that as long as they had a doctor to say Elizabeth was deluded, they would be covered. They were wrong. If a doctor had said this, it would mean that what they had been saying had caused damage and consequently would be slander. That is, they were covered against slander because they couldn't get a doctor to support them.

As for them being deliberately misleading and saying the doctor shared his concern with Mrs Bent about her mental health without adding at the same time, 'But for a completely different reason', it's as though two doctors shared their concern about a patient's physical health without mentioning that one was an eye specialist and the other was concerned about a broken bone. There are so many different kinds of mental illnesses –alcoholism, claustrophobia, nervous breakdowns, eating disorders, drug addiction, the list goes on and on, as it does with physical illnesses.

It could almost be called lying, maybe even defamation, not to state clearly what sort of mental illness a doctor is talking about. It's another example of, 'a truth told with bad intent can beat all the lies that hell can invent.' Elizabeth couldn't see how a doctor could have a valid opinion at all when at least two social workers had been proved to be liars and the notes were in such a mess.

Even if they had got a doctor's support, Elizabeth doubted very much if it would matter. She felt certain an opinion like that would be flawed. An expert witness, a psychologist, could be brought forward to give an opinion and say what their motive might be - for example, to curry favour with a social worker. Although in this story the doctors have all behaved professionally, a bad egg is bound to turn up from time to time. Bear in mind that a mental illness goes on for a long time and a patient will see a lot of them. It's not how mad the doctor is that matters, it's what form it takes.

When Elizabeth first had her nervous breakdown, her own doctor became so mentally ill that he had to be put into a nursing home. He had a brain tumour, and died from it when he was still young. The psychiatrist had an eating disorder, and he also died of his condition. Yet no one had any complaints about him either, and he cured Elizabeth.

There was a doctor who said he believed that whether or not a mental patient ever got better depended upon how they were treated when they first broke down. Elizabeth agreed. It must be particularly dangerous to have rogue doctors or mentally-ill social workers around when a patient first cracks up.

When Social Services drove Elizabeth and her mother out of their home, they said that the MP had expressed concern in a letter for the state of Elizabeth's mind, but no one could find the letter. Only Social Services saw it. In Elizabeth's case, they said it was necessary to do an assessment on her mental health. They passed it on to a CAT (Community Action Team) officer who filled in a form saying an assessment for social workers' support and assistance was necessary, that it had been referred to by her MP and that she was a schizophrenic who lived alone.

From what Elizabeth saw in his letters, the MP was trying to get them to correct her notes, and in particular the notes about the alleged compulsory admission to hospital. The director told him Elizabeth was to ask her own doctor about it. Although it was true that it was a medical matter, Elizabeth still thought he said this to mislead. It was to make him think that Mrs Bent hadn't made a mistake. The doctor explained nothing to Elizabeth, though he did to her solicitor. He told him there had never been any compulsory admission to hospital.

When the solicitor spoke to Elizabeth about it on the phone he was barking like a sergeant major. She couldn't half tell that he'd been in court when the truth comes out about someone. He was saying how much time they would be given to correct it and apologise. Elizabeth wished he'd been there when Paul Stalker went off with all her mail and Mrs Bent said he hadn't.

The director made no attempt to stick up for Elizabeth when talking to her MP about her. She didn't say anything like 'People like her are vulnerable and so often their unbelievable stories turn out to be true.' On the contrary - she ran her down. She said, 'Clearly she has a personality disorder.' She had no right to make this diagnosis - no one could find where a doctor had said so. That statement was either improper because she had no clinical evidence, or she'd been in possession of some medical records she had no business to see.

Elizabeth doubted it would matter if a doctor had said this as it could so easily be flawed. This is how a friend put it in a letter to Social Services:

As far as I can ascertain from the records, no member of the medical profession supported your view concerning her mental health. This may have been fortunate. Had they done so, as the foregoing suggests, you might have been under suspicion for causing anxiety and depression. Alternatively, Elizabeth and others may have concluded that there was some collusion between persons in authority (viz yourselves and such doctors who 'agreed' with you) deliberately acting to Elizabeth's disadvantage.

Another point is that had you been able to get their support, Elizabeth might have been able to get a case for slander. Would it be going by what you told them? Where are the letters you say she wrote?

...It seems unfortunate that the Director of Social Services wrote to the MP with the opinion that the only help Elizabeth needed was psychiatric and social. This view was contradicted by everyone else. Her solicitor's contrary opinion, and that can have some bearing, seems particularly significant given the matter was political and legal rather than medical.

Now unable to live in her own home, Elizabeth went to see her MP in the House of Commons. He didn't want to know their address in London in case it got out and he was blamed for it - he had been blamed for that once before. Clearly he didn't think there was much the matter with her, as he made no attempt to persuade her to go back home. He knew social workers were there waiting for her. The director had written in a letter to him 'We will monitor the case, awaiting her return.'

While 'on the run' they had a dreadful time staying in hostels. Elizabeth's nightmares were so bad that sometimes other people in the room would wake her up. They also became victims of crime. One man was taking £20 notes out of her handbag, but the police managed to make him pay some of it back. Another man took Mrs Elders' cheque book and was writing out cheques to himself, but a court ordered him to pay the whole lot back. It was difficult to find somewhere nice to settle.

She did meet someone she liked, a woman called Jenny, who had been reduced to a complete wreck by a nervous breakdown.

Although she was now partly recovered she was still quite nervy. She was now suffering from bereavement, as her mother had just died. She'd had to get out of the flat where they'd been living because of it, as she wasn't the leaseholder.

Jenny had had her first nervous breakdown on leaving school at 18, 20 years before. She was certain that bullying had caused it. She had been in the care of the mental health team, with regular counselling for 20 years. It wasn't the other girls but the teachers. It was the same thing Elizabeth had had with Social Services; they didn't want her to do well, they wanted control. The drive to get control can override everything. A control freak will always find a way to blame the child.

Jenny had been brainwashed into believing that she was an idiot and a failure. 'I just cannot succeed in doing anything now' she told Elizabeth. Damage like that can be very difficult to undo. Yet there were things she did enjoy. She liked walking and would help others by taking their dogs out for a walk. She liked to read and sometimes she did a bit of swimming.

Elizabeth wouldn't hear a word said against the teachers at her own school –it certainly wasn't they who had taken away her confidence. In contrast, Jenny wouldn't hear a word said against her mental health team, including the social workers.

Jenny then got a message that she could go back to the flat, as an aunt of hers had managed to take over the lease and move in. It was quite a big flat with three bedrooms, and as the aunt was allowed to sub-let there was room for Jenny, Elizabeth and her mother. It was a safe place for them to stay. It was on a high level, so they could look down and see life going on with everyone rushing round but knowing they had no part to take in it. They found this quite relaxing.

Jenny then invited another friend round, Edna. She wanted to introduce Elizabeth to her as Edna too had had dreadful trouble with abuse of the Mental Health Act. She had been put into a mental hospital largely on the basis of hearsay. Yet there was so much they could have so easily looked into. Edna's daughter had been very involved. She had made big claims about how much she cared about her mother, but soon disappeared when questions were asked, particularly about her motives. It emerged that quite a bit of money was involved. It also came out that she had told nothing like the whole truth, had deliberately misled in other ways and had told a lie. Edna had said at the time there had been no social worker present, then later when told which one he had been she said she thought he was a plain-clothes police officer, who never spoke to her and spent the whole time in the next room talking to the police. Elizabeth couldn't be certain this was true but she knew that it all too easily could be. She also knew that it would most certainly be in breach of the Mental Health Act as they are supposed to interview them.

The Elders couldn't stay at Jenny's indefinitely, and eventually they returned home. They found a letter waiting for them saying a social worker would be round next day, so they had to leave again very early the next morning. Social Services' reaction to this was to say 'There is concern that Elizabeth is dragging her mother up and down the country.'

Chapter Eight

LODGER TROUBLE

When their lodger left, the Elders found a new one, a man called Don, and this choice proved to be a disaster. Don turned out to be a 'recovering' alcoholic who was not recovering at all. He went back to drinking shortly after moving in. When he started making threats to kill Elizabeth it recalled Paul Stalker having done something very similar a while ago. He knew how much support Mrs Bent had given Stalker and that she had also given full support to Elizabeth's brother-in-law when he had been violent to her. Most important, he knew that the whole department had it in for her because she had complained about one of them.

A lot of landladies don't know how much trouble they can save themselves by nipping things in the bud. You only know when you fail and something goes wrong. But Elizabeth was afraid to begin to try. She would be discriminated against, and when things mounted up she'd be blamed for it.

She did once hear Don say to the police, 'She says it about everyone, she says it about the police' and at that time she hadn't said anything about them at all. It was because he was saying things like this that she was afraid to do anything. The whole house would stink of alcohol, and Don would vomit on the floor and leave it for her to clean up. He did far more than that, for they would have some of the most terrific rows.

She also found out that he was a transvestite, because twice she had come in and seen him coming out of her room wearing one of her flowery skirts and her mother's hat. She didn't fully realise until she found her high heeled shoes split up the sides. He had cut them with scissors to get them on.

She went upstairs to have it out with him. He denied it aggressively and said it was not her make-up he had in his room. Elizabeth had heard that transvestites can be quite pleasant people, but not this one.

The third time a pair of her knickers went missing from the bathroom she was certain Don had taken them. She went upstairs to have it out with him. He admitted he had taken them and said 'I'll give them back to you in a minute'.

'Now' she said, 'I want them back now!' and she held out her hand for him to give them her. Then she realised what his problem was. She went into the next room. He followed her in shortly after and gave them to her. He had been wearing them.

But it wasn't that, or the continual smell of alcohol, that made her finally tell him to go. It was things like interfering with phone calls she was getting, demanding to know who it was, or borrowing her bicycle and leaving it outside to be stolen. He simply would not behave as she wanted, however nicely she asked.

She feared it would finish up in some catastrophe, and when he finally set the house on fire it very nearly did. The fire brigade soon put it out, but it still made a dreadful mess of her kitchen. One of the people in the house had been so terrified that he had broken a tiny window with the hopeless idea of jumping out through it. Of all the things Elizabeth pleaded with Don about, the most important was to leave the key near the back door - in case of fire.

When she did finally tell him to go, he threatened to make up stories about her to tell Mrs Bent. 'You know what that'll mean for you don't you?' he said. Indeed she did. She also knew that it would be very difficult for her to report anything to the police, for even if they did take her side he would still be able to go crying to Social Services about it.

Then he said he would go if she gave him £500. After that he tried to tell her to leave herself, saying 'I'm not getting out, it's you that's going, I'm staying.' He continued with his threats about Mrs Bent. Mrs Elders said 'If we gave you the money you'd take it and then not go.' Elizabeth was determined not to give in to him, yet in the end she did indeed have to go. A neighbour came round to the house and said, 'I have to tell you I have just seen Don and he says he's going to kill you.' He had also said he was going to kill the neighbour.

Elizabeth invited the man into the sitting room, made certain the door was locked and started telling him what problems she was having with Don. Then suddenly the door started rattling. Don thought she was in there on her own and was trying to break his way in. It was shaking so much that she could see the hinges moving and thought they were going to break.

His tone was murderous. 'I'm coming in there to kill you, I'm going to kill you, kill you' he roared, but when the neighbour called out, 'Don, what are you doing you lunatic?' he left.

She left the house that night with her mother. They had found somewhere safe to go, but it took her about three days to calm down. Then she went to see a solicitor about getting him out. She didn't mention the threats to kill because she thought they were a civil matter, not a criminal one, and didn't want to run up any big bills. In any case, she was so used to being told there was nothing she could do about it and then getting a lot of interference from social workers. Her only interest was to get back to leading a normal quiet life.

The solicitor told her she should soon be able to get rid of him with a court order, and in fact Don telephoned him shortly after to say he'd be gone by December 19th. However he didn't go. Instead he sent a friend to where she was staying to negotiate about the money. She told the friend she was not giving Don anything.

Eventually the court case did cost her money, as Don seemed to have a calculated plan to run her into as much debt as possible. He continued to rant and rave about social injustice, the filthy rich and the poor, Elizabeth and her solicitor being examples of the rich. He phoned the solicitor and said; 'You're making a nice lot of money out of this aren't you?' and the solicitor replied, 'I wouldn't make anything at all if you'd get out.'

Of course Don would never take into account when complaining about his poverty that it wasn't everyone who got through a bottle of whisky every morning before breakfast.

So the cat-and-mouse game continued. 'I'll be gone by tomorrow' he would say, but tomorrow never came. Elizabeth would keep putting off the court case; she was terrified of having to go to such a place. He was making terrible threats of what he was going to stand up and say about her. She even feared it might get into the newspapers. When she phoned them up, sure enough, they told her they could publish anything if it was said in any court of law open to the public.

Neighbours were giving her hope by saying, 'Don't bother, he'll be snuffing it soon in any case.' And he had also made some self-pitying suggestions that he would kill himself. Then she came in one day and found a piece of paper downstairs which looked like a suicide note. It said, 'This is all your fault.' When she went upstairs she could hear deep breathing coming out of his room, as though he was in a deep sleep, maybe going into a coma, but a couple of days later she saw him riding his bicycle down the road as large as life. Don was waiting for his £500 before leaving. He would talk as if the money was his by right.

Yearning to live in her own home again, Elizabeth would sometimes creep back there, but Don would continue with his old tricks. One was to lock her out. She once gave someone else the key to go round and get something for her but he only came back with, 'I can't get in.' It seemed Don had put an extra lock on the door, yet when they went to have a look, they could see no trace of it. Maybe he had just pushed some big piece of furniture up against it, perhaps a chest of drawers.

She tried getting a male friend to mind her, but this had to stop after she had a letter from some official about it. Don had made a complaint that she was harassing him. The letter said she could have a big fine to pay, or go to prison.

There was one big difference between this letter and the reports from Social Services. They made it clear they were going entirely by what Don was saying. They also gave her the telephone number of someone she could go to if she wanted someone to defend her. But Elizabeth wasn't risking it. She was so used to people who were supposed to be on her side letting her down.

She did though, in a rage, nearly kick his door down. 'Don't you ever dare get any more letters like that sent to me!' She screamed at him. It was just luck that he was far too drunk to retaliate. He was crawling all over the floor, very, very drunk. A book case fell over, so she picked up a book from it and chucked it at him. 'Understand - no more letters like that!' she said. She had a sore throat next day from shouting so much. It worried her that the neighbours might have heard.

Then she found a simple way of dealing with him – she just crept quietly up to his room and locked him in. He slept so much that it would take him a bit of time to realise it had happened. For a while she didn't live in such fear of him suddenly descending upon her. There was some terrible banging when he realised he was locked in, followed by a terrible row, so she could only do it if she had a dog with her.

Most of the time she went to stay in the house round the corner. One night when she was there she received a phone call from a neighbour saying that Don was on his way over. He had just smashed one of her windows and was kicking cars in the road. She wasn't surprised. She had just told him she wasn't going to give him the £500. The neighbour had telephoned the police, so she phoned them too. The police told her a third person had reported it, and as she could hear her address being spoken in the background she believed they intended to do something about it. They sent a police officer round, and both she and her mother told him they had heard Don make threats to kill her. Why she had faith in them for a change she didn't know, but she went to bed in the front room downstairs and went into a deep sleep.

She awoke with a jolt at four in the morning and sat upright in bed. Something had woken her. She looked at the window, through the curtains she could see the silhouette of a man looking in at her. She hardly dared to breathe as she crept so slowly up to it to draw the curtains back to see who it was. He quickly dashed away, but she was certain it was Don. She went to phone the police, praying they would tell her it couldn't be, they had dealt with him, but they said no such thing. They said it was a landlord/tenant situation and they weren't going to do anything. They believed Don when he said he had smashed the window because he was locked out, yet it wasn't a window through which he could get in. They didn't even bother to tell her they weren't going to do anything about him. If they had, she could have gone somewhere else to stay.

She wondered how much Social Services were behind it. Had they said to the police, 'Leave it to us, we want control'?

The next day her neighbour Elsie came round, telling her to forget any idea that the police would do anything. It seemed it wouldn't have bothered them if Elizabeth or Mrs Elders had been murdered that night. Elizabeth had worked in geriatric units. She had seen nurses seriously upset a patient, leave them quite traumatised, and then come on next morning, find them dead and not be sorry for what they had done. She felt certain it would be the same with the police. If either she or her mother had been murdered they would merely have cleared away the bodies, done any other bits and bobs that needed doing after a murder, which wouldn't be much as they'd know who'd done it, and then gone off to a football match or a dance.

Then Elizabeth heard that it was against the law to make threats to kill someone, so she got the police in again next day. Another waste of time. They went upstairs to see Don, telling her to stay downstairs. When they had spoken to him they explained to her what his rights were. She was suspicious, but afraid to say anything because she had this label and felt anything she said would be interpreted as paranoia.

She became more suspicious that Social Services had something to do with it. She wondered if the police had agreed to support them instead of her. She didn't want to say anything if it was drawing unnecessary attention to it. Maybe they didn't know she had this label. Maybe her asking too many questions would be telling them.

When she told them there was nowhere nearby for her to go to, one of them told her, 'I happen to know you own several houses near here you can go to'. He was calling her a liar, but it was obvious that someone had lied to him. Elizabeth was very shocked at a police officer so casually calling a victim of crime a liar. However, as she continued to find them so daunting, she denied it very quietly. He didn't argue.

The officer also made mention of her ex-husband. What had give him the idea that she had been married? He looked completely baffled. Just what were those social workers telling him about her? It would have suited Social Services if she had been married and left her husband. It would mean they could one day get control over her. They wouldn't want a husband to be the nearest relative. He would put a stop to whatever they were doing. They'd always thought the sister would be the next of kin after her mother was dead - she'd agree to anything they said.

When Elizabeth said to the police about Don 'Clearly he's not right', they replied that he was saying the same thing about her. They regarded it as her word against his, but as she had the good character witnesses and he the bad ones, as with Paul Stalker, surely it was she who should be given the benefit of the doubt.

She said, 'You know alcoholics are notorious for it, they are bigger liars than drinkers.' They did know and were very well aware it was a very insulting thing to say to her.

As they were leaving she cried out to them, 'Please don't leave me alone with him, I have witnesses who have heard him say he's going to kill me. He's vicious, please don't leave me alone to be murdered!'

She was sobbing in fear and crying for her life, but they walked out of the door with arrogant, hard looks on their faces. Elizabeth started to feel convinced that Social Services were behind it, that the police had agreed with them to leave her alone in the house with Don, so terrified that it wouldn't take long to break her. She would very soon 'volunteer' to Social Services for 'help' and then they'd have control. The police knew that legally Social Services couldn't force her to accept it, so they must have agreed to assist them in getting it another way. If this was their idea, it went very wrong. It got to the point where she accepted that she was going to be killed, as a soldier accepts that he's going to be killed in a battle against the odds.

Then Elsie came round again. She took some pictures out of the house, as the police had refused to do anything to stop Don smashing them. She brought her dog in for protection but had to stop doing this, as even the dog got frightened of Don.

The police refused to do anything to stop him continually going off with her mother's television. They said it had to be taken from the house. She couldn't even get them interested after she told them he'd said he had put electric wires all round it and if anyone touched it they would get an electric shock. Until then she would go into his room, take it back and give it to her mother. He would then immediately go into her mother's room and take it back again. Then one day she was arguing with him about it just outside his door. He didn't know she had a big man with her on the other side. The big man came in and said, 'Excuse me mate but I've come for this television' picked it up and gave it back to her mother. After this he never took it again. It turned out that none of the wires had been electrified at all.

Don felt it was social injustice that Mrs Elders had a television and he hadn't. When a neighbour later heard about it he said, 'I wish I had known that was what all the noise was about, I've got an old television I could have let him have.'

The police also refused to do anything about him opening Mrs Elders' post, even when he took a cheque for £1100. He went round to where they were staying, and smiling all over his face, said, 'I've got a real good bit of news here, and I'm a bit short of money myself.' He was still convinced that Elizabeth was going to give him £500. She snatched it out of his hand and closed the door in his face. She had a man standing behind her at the time.

It was also suspected that he had taken Mrs Elders' post office book. They wrote a letter between them to the police about it but it was treated as a symptom of Elizabeth's supposed mental health illness, and was passed on to Social Services, the Mental Health Department, behind her back. She did ask, 'What are you doing with the letters?' but they refused to tell her. They had agreed to keep it secret from her that they had got them. She found out when they turned up in her file.

It was very tricky. If she didn't insist that things were written down they could make up what she'd said. But if she did insist, they would say it was not 'normal behaviour'. Bear in mind, Social Services can make up what a letter says, because they don't have to show it to anyone.

When she talked about this she found a lot of people don't like the police and some actively hate them. It wasn't this that surprised her, it was the fact that it was often the law-abiding and conventional types who were against them. When she said this to the police sergeant he said, 'I think it's only in your circles that people don't like us.' She never found out which circles he meant by that.

When she told them she'd write a book about them, the sergeant said, 'You can publish the name of any police officer you like and which department he works in'. What he meant was 'Everybody knows you're crackers and I mean to upset and insult you with it.' The police just refused to treat her as a sensible person. In fact, the only time they began to do so was when they asked her if she was on any medication. There are some people who remain stable with it but are completely deranged without, but Elizabeth wasn't one of them. She had proved time and time again that she didn't need drugs.

She faked surprise. 'What sort of medication might that be, I mean do I limp?'

He admitted he meant drugs for psychiatric conditions. 'Whatever makes you think such a thing?' she said. He told her it was the nature of the letters he'd seen she'd written, but it was Social Services who had told him.

'But you are not a psychiatrist' she said. 'You haven't got the right to make such a judgement! If someone has told you something untrue about me I need to know so that I can see a solicitor about slander.'

He refused to tell her. 'I think it's slander some of the things you've been saying about us' he replied. But it turned out he was ignorant. He didn't know what the word meant. He thought it was another word for insulting someone. It was a very serious lie the police sergeant told her, that it was the nature of the letters that were making him think she was mental – it wasn't. Social Services had told him. It was risking her life. If she had known this, she could have put a stop to it. She could have seen a solicitor about slander, and a criminal lawyer who would have insisted that the police assisted her.

If the police believed she should be on medication, it would at least explain one thing - why they were so gullible when they were told she was mentally ill, while clearly she was stable. Had they been told she was one of these people who needed drugs, and that without them she would become a complete lunatic?

If a lot of people are complaining about someone's behaviour and you are very surprised, it may simply be that you have never seen that person when they've been drinking. In the case of Elizabeth, if Social Services did tell the police that she was in need of medication, then that wasn't the only thing they had been seriously misinformed about.

Much later Elizabeth said to Social Services, 'Well done. You've managed to get the police and me hating one another.' Indeed they had. They had also managed to get the police to behave very badly. Elizabeth said to the police sergeant, 'You are a bad policeman. You are supposed to be able to deal with the biggest criminals and you can't even manage me.'

In the middle of all this, the police made a mistake. They turned up at the house looking for someone missing from hospital, someone who was on a section. They got the wrong place. On what pile of papers were they putting Elizabeth's address? How come there was such a suspicious mix-up?

One night when she went out for a drink she found, standing at the bar getting the rounds in, a man called Ted, a notorious alcoholic. He was saying how he only very occasionally had a drink himself. She had heard him say more than that before. It was so obvious that he was either telling a big lie or greatly deceiving himself. This was not the case with Social Services or the police. Their lie may have been just as big, but it was far more dangerous. That was when they were making the claims that their interest was for Elizabeth and her mother. People needed to know more about it, they needed to know what their motive might be and how very open to abuse the Mental Health Act was. Otherwise they might wonder if there was some other explanation.

Elizabeth went home very frightened that night. When Ted was saying all this he wasn't doing any harm to anyone else but himself. But in the case of Social Services and the police, it was thoroughly dangerous. Elizabeth found it ironic that her life could be in so much danger because the Mental Health Act was so full of statements that anything could be done if it was considered 'in the interests of the patient.'

She should have seen a criminal lawyer, but that would have been a very expensive and complicated way of dealing with it. What's needed is an amendment to the Mental Health Act, something simple and straightforward to protect the patient from this abuse.

How unfortunate that Social Services misled the police so completely. They thought Elizabeth was someone they could handle as roughly as they liked. Perhaps they thought they were all gods together, and felt insulted that she had dared to cross another god, another uniform.

Although the police didn't check up with the witnesses who heard Don make threats to kill her, a barrister interviewed them later - a criminal lawyer who was an expert in police brutality. He said, 'It's the sort of thing that reaches High Court.' He said that if he had known at the time he would first have referred her to an expert in defamation, and second insisted that the police assisted her. One of these witnesses later wrote in a letter: 'Clearly you have suffered at the hands of a woefully inadequate investigation, and also very poor information given to the police by Social Services. Clearly they have made an error.' The error was all in aid of Mrs Bent.

Jack the Ripper murdered five prostitutes in Whitechapel, East London, and was never caught. One of the theories is that two of the girls were killed by a woman, a midwife. That would explain why she went unnoticed in the street with blood on her. It's also believed she was doing abortions. These girls knew things about her which were confidential. Did she take the opportunity? There has been another theory, largely based on hearsay, that a police officer's nephew was involved in some way, maybe even that he was the Ripper. The police wouldn't want that to come out about them and especially if, I believe, it was a police officer of quite high rank. They would rather risk another girl being murdered than face up to the fact that a high-ranking officer could have a nephew who would do such a thing. Nothing has changed in the century since.

Chapter Nine

ESCAPE

One day Social Services visited a house where the Elders were staying with Scott, an artist. Scott was not very successful, but he had made enough to keep himself. He had no mortgage to pay off, no family to keep and he didn't have expensive tastes. He didn't need much. Scott was a very good-looking man and Elizabeth found him very attractive.

Naturally she was desperate to make sure Scott didn't find out that she had a psychiatric history. She feared it would interfere with her chances of marriage. He had been with a woman before who had suffered mental illness and had said 'never again'. But she was confident that he would not suspect her history. She had been better for such a long time, and everyone assumed she'd always been sane. He could only find out if someone told him.

He knew she didn't like social workers, but believed that any dealings she had with them were on account of her mother. He was willing to believe she had found them thoroughly corrupt. He knew it was a bent world we live in, and promised he would never let them inside the house.

But when Elizabeth came to the house one day, she found that some social workers had tricked their way in. They hadn't told Scott they were social workers initially, but once they were inside they told him they were from the Mental Health Team and needed to see Elizabeth. Then they went on to talk as though she was completely deranged. They said, 'We have no intention of having her sectioned.' As though they could! As if it was up to them alone, and as easy as pressing a button. Scott was amazed. He knew Elizabeth wasn't sectionable. He knew they were up to something.

It might have been lucky for them as well as for Elizabeth that Scott realised this. If he had accepted what they were saying, that Elizabeth wasn't normal, and acted upon it - for example if he had turned Elizabeth and her mother out of the house - it would have done real damage. Elizabeth would have had a case against Social Services for slander.

Elizabeth immediately left through the back door with her mother, but the social workers followed. Scott was furious. He stood between them and the door and said, 'What are you doing in my kitchen?' They looked straight at him and one of them said 'She's written to her MP', as though Elizabeth had done something very wrong.

Scott got out of the way. He could see a fight breaking out. He could see himself getting mixed up in an assault case.

Elizabeth and her mother got the first train to London and she telephoned him from there. He said, 'I've told them not to come again' as though that was that, but she thought she would let him find out for himself that they wouldn't take any notice of that. He soon did - they phoned him up and told him that he wasn't free to ban them from his house if he had Elizabeth and her mother living there.

'I'm just not having it' said Scott. 'I'm not having people I don't want inside my house. I'll fight them on the beaches if I have to!' He sounded like Sir Winston Churchill. So Elizabeth and her mother went back.

Sometimes Mrs Elders would fall and injure herself. Although

Elizabeth always took her to the hospital, she never had any peace of mind, because Don was saying, 'I'm going to tell the social workers I saw you giving her a push.' She knew Social Services would listen to that; they'd want to hear it. Once, when one of the neighbours was sweeping up some of the blood outside her house, she said she thought there'd been a dog fight, but then another neighbour told her she'd seen Mrs Elders go over. If only Elizabeth could have some say in which witnesses they checked up with.

A little later she decided to give them another chance. Perhaps they would look into her side of the story. Another neighbour had just complained that Don had been lying flat on his back at her front gate, kicking his legs up in the air, and she couldn't get past to do her shopping. She said, 'Tell those social workers to come and see me if they say he wasn't there.' So Elizabeth phoned them up. She spoke to Mrs Maffee, but all she would say was, 'We'll come round and have a little chat about it.' She told her she wouldn't check up on any of the witnesses. 'We use our own judgement' she said. Elizabeth wasn't having that. She later found out how they made that one out; it states in the Mental Health Act that they have to have an independent opinion. For example, they are not to be influenced by the police or a doctor. It's another example of how they can't tell the difference between opinion and fact. The Act doesn't mean they can decide what the facts are about a case. This neighbour didn't intend to give an opinion. She wanted to be a witness to what had happened.

Elizabeth later found out why she was so eager to come round to the house, to have 'a little chat'. If you don't know the Mental Health Act it may sound like common sense to let them inside the house, to show them how obliging you are, but if you do know it, it would make a lot of sense not to let them in. In fact you'd have to be a complete idiot to let them in, if you are experiencing very strange and bad behaviour from them. Once they've seen you face to face they have a lot more power and it will make it a lot easier for them to make up what you have done and said.

The next time Mrs Elders fell and cut her head open, Elizabeth had a witness again. A man called an ambulance, not knowing what trouble it might cause for Elizabeth. In the end, the Elders found it all too much and went to live in Dover. They managed to get lodgings in a side street near the sea, just under the famous White Cliffs of Dover. She spent all day going up and down the road to a phone box trying to get Scott on the phone, before it occurred to her that he might be on his way to see her. As it was beginning to get dark she heard his voice in the street saying 'Elizabeth, is that you?'

They got married a few days later by special licence. It reminded her of what a Jew had said in the very early days of Nazi Germany: 'I am afraid to do anything in case it's against the law for Jews'. Elizabeth was afraid to do anything because of the Mental Health Act. She was quite prepared to hear that they could stop her getting married. As Scott said later to his MP about it, 'They seemed dead against us getting married, they seemed to be doing all they could to stop it.' He didn't seem to realise that they had a motive for that. It would mean he would be Elizabeth's nearest relative and could put a stop to some of the things they were doing. They were waiting for Mrs Elders to die so that Sisley would be the next of kin.

Shortly after they came back an eviction order was issued against Don. In spite of being told he'd go to prison if he was caught inside the house, he still didn't go, which was contempt of court. He and Elizabeth would be standing by the gas stove side by side, cooking their separate meals, him wearing a tight skirt and high heeled shoes; she thought he did it on purpose to annoy her. An onlooker would have thought they were the best of friends and about to sit down and enjoy a meal together.

She telephoned her solicitor, who already knew Don had not left as he had phoned the solicitor from the house, on her phone. When she came in shortly afterwards, the bailiffs had been and he'd gone. He had been highly indignant when they arrived and said, 'She was supposed to give me some money.'

How Elizabeth wished she wasn't so vulnerable and could be like everyone else. She wished she was like another landlady just a few doors away from her, who had booted her lodger out head first. But unlike Elizabeth, this other landlady wasn't open to blackmail. She had nothing to fear. When her lodger started coming in drunk, she was free to say to him 'OUT!'. But Elizabeth's lodger knew she had a psychiatric history and he could tell people about it. If Elizabeth hadn't got something to hide she would have had Don diving out of the bathroom window the first time he vomited there and left it there for her to clean up. She could have lived a normal, quiet life, the same as everyone else.

It reminded her of when Paul Stalker had been harassing her and her mother, and had sent them a very nasty Christmas card. The team leader refused to assist them in telling the police. She said Mrs Elders would be safe if she was put into a home. Safe perhaps, but desperately unhappy. She'd be yearning the whole time to go back home and live with her daughter. But whoever was in charge of the home would be able to get the police. They would be willing to assist her because her label would say 'Matron', while Elizabeth's label says 'mentally ill'.

After Don left, he burned his new lodgings down because he was so careless, and died in the fire. Elizabeth didn't hear what his new landlady had to say about that, but she felt sure she'd be absolutely furious and dancing up and down like a lunatic.

As regards Elizabeth, it was some time later when she found out how right she had been to go so far. While she was on her honeymoon, lounging about on sunny beaches, social workers were busy making up evidence about her to get her sectioned. This is what a friend of Elizabeth's wrote to another social worker:

I am writing this on behalf of Elizabeth. She can't write herself, as anything she says is interpreted as paranoia. This is not to suggest that you would do such a thing but anything you did say might be repeated as, 'Mrs X says...' etc, whether you had said it or not.'

Mrs Maffee put up a very big fight on behalf of Social Services not to have to answer questions and not to have to correct notes. She was determined to cover up what a bad social worker Mrs Bent was and to put a stop to Elizabeth's last complaint being looked into. After driving Elizabeth out of her home, Mrs Maffee had contacted Social Services in the town she'd gone to, to get them to be a party to it. She made up information in order to do so, but they were not a bit taken in. She tried it again with another mental health team when Elizabeth moved on, but this time when making up evidence she tried even harder to persuade them to put Elizabeth into a mental hospital. She said, *'Keep in touch. Let us know what happens.'*

Social Services in Grimley said in writing that they were fully justified in passing on information as they needed to *'alert them to the fact that she might be in need of their services'*. They went on: *'This is entirely in keeping with the guidance on the transference of information should a person be suffering from a serious mental illness, and with the recommendation of numerous incident enquiries, and the department could have been subject to severe criticism if it had failed to pass on the information and there had been some untoward incident involving Elizabeth and her mother in Kent.'*

Doesn't it sound convincing? A solicitor explained to me what they were saying. There had recently been a case where a man on

119

the underground had stabbed another man to death. If the local mental health team had known he had moved into their area, they might have been able to do something to avoid it. But the information wasn't passed on.

That letter wasn't libel, as it didn't do any damage. The social workers concerned immediately smelled a rat and their suspicions were then confirmed by a solicitor. Their only interest was to assure Elizabeth that they would leave her alone. They didn't even want to know who her own doctor was, and as far as they were concerned she didn't exist. They said the same as the social workers in Gorsedale: 'As long as you know where we are if you need us.'

Mrs Maffee then wrote something similar to Elizabeth's own doctor, but suggesting more strongly that she should be sectioned. She asked if they had to wait until there was a crisis, and if he could think of any reason they could give to have her sectioned. Again this wasn't libel as it didn't do any damage. The doctor knew what they were up to, but the other social workers were completely baffled.

According to the notes written by Social Services, her doctor said that 'despite the paranoiac state she is at present in' Elizabeth was a quiet person who was capable of living a normal, quiet life. We don't believe her doctor did say she was suffering from paranoia. We think they made it up. It wasn't what he said to her solicitor, it wasn't what he said to her, and he didn't say it to her nearest relative, her mother.

It's rather as though a doctor refused to do anything about a man having leprosy, saying, 'It's all right, he's not spreading germs to anyone else and it's not doing any damage to him.' People would begin to wonder if he had leprosy at all.

As regards Mrs Maffee saying, 'It seems we will have to wait until there is a crisis before we can use the powers of the Mental Health Act', the trouble was that they would cause a crisis and then blame Elizabeth. But they were never going to get their wish, because all the doctors agreed that trying to section her was not realistic.

Elizabeth was a victim of a subtle form of blackmail. When she phoned Social Services and told them not to come to the house because it was crucial that no one knew about her mental health status, and their presence was arousing suspicion, they told her they had to come. They said that if she didn't quietly let them inside the house this might well come out about her.

It all originated from Elizabeth insisting that notes should be corrected and that her complaint about Mrs Bent should be investigated. In fact, it started with a complete fantasy - Mrs Bent's dream of getting control over Elizabeth's life. Now she denies that she was asking the doctors to section her, so we will have to guess on what grounds she thought she would get it.

We think it was Mrs Maffee who later asked a psychiatrist to section her. We have seen where this psychiatrist has written in a letter to the director, *'I have not up to date been provided with any information which would make me think it would be helpful to detain her under The Mental Health Act.'*

Of course, he meant helpful to the patient. He must have known there was plenty that would have made it helpful to them.

We think that when Mrs Maffee was busy making up information, she did not know how wildly untrue it all was that Mrs Bent had written in the report or was saying about her. It's rather as though you think you know what a man has been convicted of before, so you think you know what evidence to make up to get him convicted again.

We suspect Mrs Bent made a hoax phone call to Elizabeth pretending to be someone else. She got her to send her a book to someone who she knew would complain about it. But we only say this because there seems no one else but Mrs Bent who would have a motive for doing such a thing. And it is the sort of thing she would do. It's typical of a control freak. One thing is certain – she jumped at the chance to tell the local mental health team that Elizabeth had sent this someone this book.

Mrs Elders was much happier living in Dover. She loved the gulls and could hear them calling all the time. The steps to the White Cliffs were just at the end of the road and she and Elizabeth would frequently go up them for walks along the top, sometimes getting as far as St Margaret's Bay. Everywhere there was heather, wild grasses, wild flowers, a complete wilderness, and on a clear day they could see right across the sea to France.

She had her passport with her and they were at the Gateway to Europe. They could see the boats coming in and going out. How could anyone feel more free? Yet at the same time these social workers were talking about how to separate them and put Elizabeth into a mental hospital.

Mrs Elders was now free of the power freaks, the people who had tried to control her life by making claims that their interest was in helping her. But living in Dover did bring daily reminders of the trade in animals which she despised so much. Animals were being exported every day from the end of the road and as a vegan she hated the killing and eating of animals.

Every morning she and Elizabeth would go down to the docks to see the livestock ships docking and sailing, and meet some of the people protesting. Sometimes, if it was early, they would take their breakfast down to the docks with them and eat it there.

The demonstrations were quiet and orderly. There were plenty of police about and they would be most amicable. In fact it was usually the same ones each morning, and they got to know them quite well. They were very keen on safety; they made certain no one ran in front of a lorry. They were completely different from the other police the Elders knew, whose only interest had been to curry favour with Social Services.

When it got back to Social Services in Grimley that the Elders had been attending the demonstrations, they tried to put a stop to it.

They wrote in the notes, 'We contacted Dover Social Services and told them there is concern that Elizabeth is dragging her mother to demonstrations'.

Something else happened to tell the women not only how peculiar and dreadful some people are but how far on the wrong side of the law they can get. Living halfway up the cliff was a tramp. He was old, and although he had been born in Russia he had been in Britain for years and years. He lived with his cat in a little hut there, and seemed cheerful enough, but then word got around the local thugs that if you wanted a few kicks, you went up there. After he was beaten up for the second time, the old man was forced to go and live in a home.

The Elders had another thing to remind them that some people were prepared to wreck everything for them. The cottage they rented backed on to the cliffs, and Dover Castle was right at the top of it. They frequently walked up to a museum there. Something they saw made their blood run cold. It was a photograph of some German generals with telescopes in Calais, looking across the sea at England only 21 miles away. They were dreaming of getting across and ruling us all. How they would have loved to have walked along those cliffs, looking down on it all, including the little cottage where Elizabeth and her mother were living and knowing that they had complete charge over everyone and everything.

Then she saw something else to make her blood run even colder. She saw a glimpse of a film which showed Castle Street. Now it was such a nice road to go shopping in, but it had been very different in wartime. Housewives carrying shopping baskets were dashing for the air raid shelters and German and Allied planes were up above chasing and shooting at one another. The Germans were fighting to get in and we were fighting to keep them out.

What everyone found so ridiculous was that meanwhile in

Germany, sirens were going off to warn them that we were coming to attack them. If only all of this fighting, invading and defending would stop. A nearby neighbour showed them the air raid shelter at the bottom of her garden. It had been dug into the cliff. As a child she would sleep there at night and hear it all going on above her.

Whatever is it that makes some people want to rule the world? Why do they want so much? How many people like this are there around us, and how far would they go if they could? Yet although all this is a lot more horrendous, it was still more realistic for those German generals to think they were going to get a swastika put on Buckingham Palace than it was for those social workers to imagine they were going to get Elizabeth committed.

It was much later when Elizabeth and her mother found out about events at Buckingham Palace. More and more was coming out about King Edward the Eighth. He had abdicated the throne in the 1930s as they refused to let him marry the woman he loved, Mrs Simpson. She was an American who had been divorced twice and the British said they weren't having her for their queen. Then later it emerged there was a lot more to it than that. Maybe he had intended being king one day.

During the decades that followed, rumours that Edward had connections with Nazi Germany were shown to be fact. Did he think he would be king of a Nazi Britain? Just what was he up to? To have connections at all with Germany at such a time was greatly disloyal to his family as well as his country. He was in France when Hitler marched in and he was sympathetic to the Germans. He saw the French on the streets weeping because the Germans had conquered them, and he seemed to be happy that it would be Britain next. He was prepared to let it happen to his own family. Yet as Mrs Elders read about all this and knew how wicked her own family were, she still knew that she had the family she wanted. She had Elizabeth.

* * * * * * * *

Meanwhile there was plenty more going on that Elizabeth didn't know about. Mrs Maffee was getting quite nervous, as she was not only finding out how right Elizabeth had been but also that Mrs Bent had done all this before. When she had worked in a completely different area she had been interviewed by the director of Social Services over horrendous mistakes she'd made there, and been warned that a patient might have grounds to sue them for libel. She had also been interviewed about being too officious. There had been more than one complaint that she was too ready to give out orders. Mrs Maffee wished she'd never come to that department to work and that she didn't have to work with Mrs Bent. Now she was trying to cover up for her, and one thing was certain, they must not admit how very wrong those notes were about Elizabeth Elders. She was to be brainwashed into believing they weren't wrong at all. They were also to brainwash her into believing that their interest in it was to help her.

When Mrs Bent came out of her interview, Mrs Maffee asked if she had got the sack.

'Of course I didn't!' blustered Mrs Bent, and refused to say any more about it. Clearly it had upset her, and Mrs Maffee began to get more nervous and more determined to shut Elizabeth's mouth, especially when she read something in the papers about a case where a child had been molested and the headline said he had done it before. The man they convicted had an appalling record. It mustn't get out that Mrs Bent had a history too, a history for getting everything wrong and one for being too ready to give out orders.

Then things got worse for Mrs Maffee. She was now in a real big panic. Elizabeth's solicitor was asking to see the letters that she had alleged Elizabeth had written, the letters she had used as evidence when asking the doctors to section her. Of course she couldn't produce them, because she had written them herself.

She would go over it again and again in her mind. She hadn't shown them to anyone. She had kept them to one side in case one of the doctors asked to see them. She had found forgery so easy, with cutting and pasting on computers. It had been such a temptation when Elizabeth had been insisting that everything was in writing and she wouldn't say what she wanted her to say. Yet it had seemed to solve everything to start off with. The doctors all seemed happy to take her word for it. When one of them didn't, and said he wanted to see the evidence, she had got cold feet. She didn't show him the forgery but merely said she'd find it later. He didn't ask her again.

But now what was she going to tell Elizabeth's solicitor? She would have to say she hadn't received the request. He sent reminders, and she didn't answer those either. Maybe she could say he had to accept her interpretation, but when she remembered what Elizabeth had put she knew he wouldn't accept that.

She deeply regretted what she had done. Yet there was one good thing she felt she had achieved. She had destroyed quite a number of the letters that Elizabeth had written, the letters that no one was to see. There was too much truth in them.

But Elizabeth wasn't going to give in. She wasn't going to accept any of their 'help' and Mrs Maffee was beginning to come to terms with the fact that she would not be able to use force. Elizabeth was saying she suspected forgery. Mrs Maffee wanted to stop her, to say that it was slander, but a solicitor told her she couldn't. Elizabeth was careful how she worded it.

Then they tried another one. They said Elizabeth could come in and have a look at the letters herself. They did have some left. Elizabeth wasn't having that. It would be her word against theirs what they showed her, so she went on insisting they were to be sent to either her solicitor or her doctor. The fact that she refused meant that they could now say, 'She's been told she can come and have a look, refuses to come and then complains that she's not seen them.'

They didn't mention at the same time what Elizabeth's point was, but they did use it as evidence that Elizabeth was a very difficult person to deal with. This only kept them happy for a while. Elizabeth plodded on. Eventually they did send some letters to Elizabeth's solicitor, but they were letters that Elizabeth had never denied writing.

Mrs Elders, meanwhile, was completely unaware that any of this was going on. On fine mornings she would walk along the beach and look forward to the day, feeling that she had many more to come. Indeed, she had many happy days ahead of her, though not as many as she deserved. The bus stop was just at the end of the road and she was able to go for day trips to Belgium and France and even weekends in Amsterdam. When social workers had tried to take over her life she had nearly faded away, but the roses came back to her cheeks and she laughed and sang again.

Chapter Ten

ENDINGS

They were happy years, but they were all too short. Rose Elders died six years later at the age of 90. Only Elizabeth, her husband Scott and two of her friends came to the funeral. The rest of the family had abandoned her as soon as her house had been sold and the money was gone. She had been dead for three years before they even found out. She had been the cow that had been milked all its life and then, when its use ran out, put on the rubbish heap to rot, for all they cared. They had no idea where she was. She could have been in a home somewhere, desperately unhappy.

As the coffin was driven slowly along the road, there were only two bouquets of flowers on it, but they were both from people whose feelings were deep and sincere. Elizabeth had heard so much about big funerals, with people crying and showing great hypocrisy, for they had been horrible to the person before they had died. At least there was nothing like this at Rose Elders' funeral.

A priest said to her afterwards about it, 'Well, you most certainly honoured your father and mother.' Her father's was another story, nothing like this one and one that had happened thirty years before.

Mrs Bent's dream in which she saw Mrs Elders dying and the doctor standing by her bedside telling Elizabeth she had managed admirably well - that bit of the story came true. It was because Mrs Bent feared it that she had dreamed it.

One good thing came out of the terrible things that happened to the Elders. Mrs Elders would rant and rave, 'How dare these people come round to my house and criticise and criticise my daughter like this?' but then she would turn to Elizabeth and say, 'Oh Elizabeth I'm so proud of you'. She wanted to make that clear before she went.

Was it a blessing in disguise that the rest of the family abandoned her? For there are other aspects of this story, about other relatives who have not been mentioned. Rose was left only with Elizabeth, but sometimes only one person is needed. Elizabeth cherished her, and fought for justice with her. The fact that it was so all unfair made it a lot easier for Elizabeth to devote so much time to looking after her mother. Mrs Elders had looked after young people all her life. How wrong, how unfair it would have been, if in old age there had been no one to look after her. Especially as when she'd been young she had indeed done her bit, more than her bit, of seeing to old people. She certainly did not abandon her own elderly relatives.

One Christmas Elizabeth feared her mother might be near the end, so in early December they went to Dublin and stayed in a B&B. It was not too early for them to join some people singing Christmas carols around a big Christmas tree in the city centre. The owner of the B&B didn't mind getting things in for them like Christmas pies and crackers, even though it was still three weeks to Christmas. How much her mother knew or cared about her health Elizabeth didn't know, but when they got back to England, instead of deteriorating, she got a lot better, so they went out and celebrated Christmas all over again at home. Then came the January sales, with Christmas food going for half price, so they had another Christmas. In the space of a few weeks they had three Christmases.

One thing Mrs Elders had been keen on all her life, when running round after the young and the old, was to see to it that things like birthday cards didn't get forgotten. When Elizabeth went to visit her in hospital once, all the other patients had a row of get well cards on their locker and Mrs Elders didn't have one. Yet she had loved cards so much. Elizabeth dropped a few hints about it to the neighbours, and next time she went to visit there they were, a row of get well cards on her locker.

As Rose became more frail, memories came back to Elizabeth of all the family, old aunts and grandparents, and she could tell they thought of her as only a girl. How dreadful if when Rose was old she was abandoned because everyone who had ever loved her was now dead. But it didn't happen. She wasn't abandoned by everyone, and nor did the rest of the family get away with saying she had Alzheimer's disease, or even that the assumption could be made that she had turned into a nasty old woman. Elizabeth knew they had seen a letter in which she wrote, 'Until the day she died everyone said what a lovely lady she was.

The state didn't abandon her either – at least, not the doctors or nurses. Elizabeth took her mother far from their jurisdiction, where no one knew Elizabeth had a psychiatric history, or that she had complained about another team.

Mrs Elders died in hospital and in Elizabeth's letter of thanks to the staff she wrote, 'She looked after young people all her life, and when she was old young people looked after her, so there is some justice in the world.'

* * * * * * * *

Other members of the family not mentioned in this story, who abandoned Mrs Elders when she was old, are still in touch with Paul Stalker and talk compassionately about him. They say, 'Oh poor Paul, you should be kind to him.'

Paul Stalker may only have been beating up Mrs Elders

psychologically, but he did it again and again. A misogynist will do that. The psychological damage they do can go on for years. Sometimes it is never put right. You can get people into such a mess that they can no longer work. They will get the support of all health officials on that. So why do some people stick up for the misogynist? Does it make them feel pious to be sympathetic towards him? Do they feel they need something to feel pious about because they have a guilty conscious? Elizabeth didn't know.

Her great-niece stuck up for him in a crisis, although she could so easily have helped Mrs Elders. Despite this, for the next two Christmases running, she sent her a pretty little Christmas card and present. She wrote on one of them 'with lots and lots of love.' They went straight back. Some people may think she was filled with great remorse for what she had done, but there was plenty to show otherwise. Elizabeth was certain the pretty cards were only an attempt to look sweet and caring and would never have been sent at a time when she might have been expected to do something to help.

This reminded Elizabeth of something she had read in the newspapers about a psychiatric unit. The hospital staff were criticising their patients, calling them dangerous and making claims that they had injuries from being attacked, yet at the same time they were claiming that their interest was to help them. It gave the name of the hospital and the ward they were on, open to anyone to read who knew anyone on that ward, and to guess who it was they were talking about. Let us hope they knew it can sometimes be the staff that are stirring it up, and let us especially hope they would suspect this if it was describing behaviour which was completely out of character.

Mrs Elders said when she read this: 'I think they believe all this themselves, that their interest is for the patients and not in getting sympathy from the public next time they put in for their next pay rise.' It was the union leader who did most of the slagging.

When Elizabeth telephoned the reporter who had written the piece, she admitted that she had not spoken to any of the patients. They hadn't been given a chance to defend themselves. Elizabeth said, 'Whenever I've been visiting anyone on that ward they've always looked too drugged to attack anyone'. It may not even be true they were violent before they were admitted - people with mental health problems are not usually violent. It's a dreadful shame that the staff didn't make that bit clear when talking to the papers. It would have been a wonderful chance to help their patients. There is so much ignorance and fear about mental illness, and it can do a patient a lot of damage.

In this case the newspaper reporter didn't see the book the staff were talking about; the one that was full of reports on these attacks on them. Elizabeth asked her, 'How do you know there is one?' She didn't. She had taken their word for it. Elizabeth told her she knew for a fact that on that ward the hospital authorities had refused to investigate allegations that a doctor had been violent with a patient.

* * * * * * * * * *

Sisley's husband Ronald died on the same day Elizabeth's husband came out of hospital. Now she had a husband and Sisley didn't. It was ironic that he had died of a massive heart attack, as in the days when they'd been friends she had kept them well informed of the Coronary Prevention Group.

Ronald's death must have hit Sisley like a mad truck, yet if Mrs Elders had been alive I doubt very much that she would have responded to any requests to give her any comfort. It would be too much of a risk. They had to keep away from her. She had to keep her other daughter safe. In any case Sisley was surrounded by such a large family.

Elizabeth knew of a case where a daughter had tried to kill her old mother and still the mother tried to defend her. The mother was in a home and was well settled and not unhappy there. In fact it was the home that put a stop to it. In order to get the money the daughter had been trying to persuade her to commit suicide, and they got it on camera. Oh how that mother tried to defend her daughter! First it showed a carer going into a drawer where the daughter had left some drugs for her mother to take. She was trying to stop her but the carer said, 'No dear, I've got to see what's in here.' Then the mother discovered that the man with her was a police detective. The final blow was that there was another detective outside arresting her daughter. Her daughter was under lock and key and the mother remained safe in the home. She clearly considered it to be her home. How easy it is to forgive if you are safe in a home.

Sisley's husband died the day before Guy Fawkes night. When Elizabeth had been visiting her own husband in hospital, she had described it as like a war zone. Fireworks were going off everywhere. She went outside to see if there were any in the hospital grounds. She said, 'People are dying on this ward, they don't want this racket going on while they're on their way out.' She had no idea that her brother-in-law was on his way out in another hospital miles away, and the next day she would be free from all fear of him for ever. He died just as Elizabeth was finishing a course in counselling for the bereaved.

It's a dreadful shame that Sisley had despised her since they had been children. There were so many things she could have helped her with, but it was out of the question. Firstly, Elizabeth would never have dared, and secondly, as Sisley believed she was so superior, she would think it was degrading to imagine that Elizabeth could ever be of any use. People who listened to her talking would be amazed if they knew what Elizabeth was really like. She talked as though her sister was a hopeless cabbage, a complete head-banger, and a damn nuisance to everyone, everywhere she went.

Yet no one could have loved her daughter more than Mrs Elders had. She had always been willing to do anything for Sisley and to show her that nothing was too much trouble. No one could have been a more dedicated mother than she was. Did that love die, or was she too afraid to love? We will never know. No one ever asked her.

POSTSCRIPT

*You people hate anyone who challenges injustice and speaks
the whole truth in court. You have oppressed the poor and robbed them
of their grain. - Amos 5-10*

This has been a story about Social Services, how utterly ruthless and unscrupulous some of their officers can be, how their only interest is in themselves and what liars they can be if they have something to hide. It's about how, regardless of how grossly incompetent one of them has been, their colleagues refuse to see it. Reckless is worse than careless.

'The lunatics are running the asylum', as someone said when a bunch of Hollywood actors took over the United Artists studios in the 1920s. The same comment was made by a woman who suffered at the hands of the caring services more recently. By the lunatics, she meant the staff. This is what she wrote:

I arrived home today to find my back door kicked down. The people I'd been sharing the house with had had some jeering to put up with only a few days previously. On top of this, two days before, a couple of these yobbos had actually broken the lock on the back door, got inside the kitchen, and faced one of us, Mathew, and Mathew had chased him out with a chair. I promise you readers, Mathew never started that, he's scared stiff of them.

It's surprising really how I can handle things like this because I manage quite well. I managed to get a joiner to put the back door on. He made it impossible for the door to be broken down again. Yes, I can handle these thugs who discriminate against eccentrics, these skinheads who hang about street corners or in the bus station, who will just use swear words as adjectives and aggressively so, and who will tell such lies. I also thank people who have been before us that legally they can't get very far with it. Eccentric spinsters used to be burnt to death at the stake as witches and so would other such people. It wasn't safe to be the village fool. But I cannot cope if it's a thug that's joined the medical profession. I cannot manage if it's someone professional that's discriminating against me.

The last woman to hang

Ruth Ellis, the last woman to hang in Britain, may have been another case. The man she killed and was hanged for had never been any good. He did one thing after another to show he felt nothing for her. She wouldn't leave him. She had a child of four, got a job in a pub and she and the landlady were able to sort out hours that suited them both perfectly. It meant that Ruth could both work and look after the child. That man wrecked the lot of it. After his third big row in the pub, maybe even a fight, she got the sack. He wasn't sorry at all.

It has even been doubted by some people that it was her bullets that killed him. If they did, she was a remarkably good marksman for the amount of practice she'd had. He was trying to dodge them, and was clearly very frightened when he realized he was being shot at. Some people say there was another man in the background firing too, a man who hated him and was capable of putting Ruth Ellis up to it.

There's another point here which I believe may be typical of women in cases of misogyny. Did Ruth Ellis think it was pious to stand by that man? She did write in a letter to his parents, "I died loving your son". That sounds like someone from a drama. Maybe she saw herself as some sort of a movie star.

The Brides in the Bath

Then there was another case, Joseph Smith and the story known as the 'Brides in the Bath'. Bessie Mundy, one of the three girls he drowned, was extraordinarily gullible. She wrote in a letter to her uncle about her 'health' problem, her supposed epilepsy, her fits which only her husband saw. She wrote 'I have made out a will and left everything to him. This is only right as he has been extremely kind'. Did he just dictate that letter to her, and did Paul Stalker just dictate to Mrs Bent what to write in the notes about Elizabeth? Joseph Smith also got her to tell her doctor she was having fits. He was making plans to drown her in the bath and make it look like an accident.

How did it all happen? Why were Bessie Mundy and the other women so taken in? He would get engaged within days of meeting them and then take out an insurance policy on them. However did this poorly-educated man, rough and nasty with it, manage so quickly to get these middle-class, genteel women to so quickly agree to marry him and to be insured by him?

Jeremy Bamber

This is a case where the police didn't want to know all the evidence, because they could so easily blame someone who was mental. They were extraordinarily gullible. When Bamber phoned to say his sister had gone mad with a gun, killing the whole family and then herself, they quickly got rid of many clues to an alternative explanation and completely overlooked the fact that Bamber had a motive for doing it himself – money.

First, it was physically impossible for the sister, Sheila Caffell, to have killed herself as Bamber claimed. The silencer for the shotgun was too long and her arms were too short to allow her to point the gun at her own head. The silencer must have been used to kill her as it had her blood on it, yet it had been removed and placed in a cupboard after her death. Also, she was shot twice – you can't fire a second shot when you have already killed yourself with the first.

After a murder the police have a lot of work to do and it's easy to say it was suicide, but I think it's a lot deeper than that. Why bother, if someone involved has a psychiatric history? You just blame them.

It appears that the police here were as incompetent as Mrs Bent. The mistakes started at the top of page 1 and went on from there. The judge heavily criticised the police chief in charge of the case.

Within his first few sentences, Jeremy Bamber made a claim that was impossible - that his father had phoned him and said 'Please come over, your sister's gone crazy and she's got a gun', and then dropped the phone when attacked. Bamber told the police he had redialled after the phone went dead and had got the engaged tone. Yet if his father had dropped the receiver, the line would have stayed open. His son could not have obtained a dialling tone until either the receiver had been replaced or two units of phone time had been automatically metered – which would have been 10 minutes at that time of night. This fact alone undermined Bamber's story.

When the police found Nevill Bamber dead beside the phone, it was clear from his injuries that he had been struggling for his life. He would hardly have had much of a fight if it had been Sheila Caffell who attacked him, as she was a slight woman and he was a big man, 6ft 4in tall. In any case Sheila's body bore no traces of a fight.

But as far as the police were concerned, it was a clear case of a madwoman at work. They did not take the fingerprints they should have done and were not, for example, told to wear gloves when handling the rifle. Many parts of the building were not searched properly and the silencer was left for the family to find. Bloodstains were washed from a wall, and bloodstained bedding and carpets were removed from Bamber's bedroom and burned, along with other possible evidence.

When the police spoke to the villagers, they heard what they wanted to hear – that she was, as Bamber had said, a 'complete nutter'. Yet later the village folk told reporters that they were surprised that the police had been so certain that Sheila Caffell was the killer. It was news to them that Sheila knew how to fire a gun, let alone reload a rifle twice and fire a total of 25 shots.

Later Julie Mugford, Bamber's girlfriend, told the police that he had told her of his plans to drug his parents and set fire to the farmhouse. He even told her after the police arrived 'I should have been an actor'.

* * * * * * * * *

Robert Mugabe, the Zimbabwean President, said 'I wouldn't tell a lie and if ever I cheated I would have it on my conscience, I wouldn't be able to sleep at night'. That was despite overwhelming evidence that he did far more than lie, he rigged elections. I would say some public officials in Britain are as deluded as Mugabe. What everyone else calls gross incompetence they call great efficiency. If they believe that, or that it is not normal behaviour to complain about them, they are as deluded as Mugabe.

Several of us put an advertisement in a left-wing magazine to see if other people had experienced anything similar. We had plenty of answers. We also saw their notes. In one case they started off with the patient's psychiatric history, then went on to talk as though their complaint had been mere paranoia. In the very next sentence, as though it was a continuation of her illness, the doctor said, *'Recently she has focused her attention on what she believes to be a campaign by her relatives to have her signed away into a mental hospital. It can be difficult to distinguish whether these claims have some basis as I have received phone calls from relatives requesting that she should be sectioned.'*

It may be difficult for the doctor to distinguish as he's biased, she's complained about the service, but it is blatantly obvious to everyone else. If someone phones up and says 'Will you section my mother?' then obviously they are trying to get her sectioned.

How can we manage, if our ministers are capable of being as deluded as Mugabe? I have had so much experience of it with various health officials and the ministers in Parliament. When they were revising the Mental Health Act 1983, they would assure me there would be plenty of safeguards, and I would breathe a sigh of relief and think the nightmare would soon be over and I would be able to forget all about it. That was until I found out what the safeguards were going to be - an appeal after the patient had already been committed. I cannot get them to accept that a patient must be accepted as innocent before they are put away, not after, when it's too late and the damage has been done.

Another authority wrote to say: *'If that person disagrees with the reasons given by the social worker for application before admission, then there's no legal means under current law to challenging this before admission.'* They when went on to say: *'After admission a person can apply to a Mental Health Review Tribunal, which gives them an opportunity to put their views forward to an independent body'.* It's another example of how they can't tell the difference between views and facts. I didn't write in about disagreeing with opinions, I wrote in about facts not being correct.

They kept writing to tell me they'd get their officers better trained - I couldn't get them to understand that I am not talking about lack of training. That was not the problem here. Deliberately misleading people by not telling the whole truth is not lack of training – it's corruption.

Several of us concluded that the ministers were in denial when we saw a suggestion put forward by them: *'Three will have to sign before any compulsory measures can be taken, and that will ensure all circumstances will be looked into.'* That may be a normal assumption for some people to make, but it wasn't for them. They've been given example after example of how a whole team can go wrong.

What's up with the ministers and the health officials? 'Bollocks' explained one woman when she heard it. I think she felt insulted after all the examples she'd given them and wanted to insult them in turn.

Why won't they admit to it? Do they think they may one day be vulnerable, at the mercy of health officials, and are anxious not to offend them? They haven't even thought they could all be going by the same history, and the history has been written by someone like Mrs Bent.

A hysterical history like the one which she wrote about Elizabeth may be started by a middle-aged woman who is jealous of young girls, or it may not be that at all. Perhaps a patient has a good-looking wife and the doctor is jealous. The list of possible motives goes on and on.

Of course a doctor is quite right in making certain a patient knows that three people have got to sign. They must not think that he alone has all this power. But if a doctor, after being told fully by a patient about their history, and with evidence to support it, said to that patient that nothing could go wrong, that doctor is in denial.

I have already compared this case with that of Dr Shipman. He killed so many victims because people were afraid to suggest that a man in his position could do anything wrong. A young undertaker had reported that she was more than suspicious. She said, 'Yet again I have been asked to go and pick up a body, yet again there is no sign of there having been any illness in the house, yet again Dr Shipman is the doctor attending'. But Shipman was allowed to go on killing.

Then there was Dr Robert Clements. In 1939, after his third wife died, people began to get suspicious. Nothing was done about it. 'What a thing to say about a doctor!' they said. 'Who could suggest such a thing!' One woman doctor did – she complained about it repeatedly. She had to give in, saying 'Very well, we shall just have to wait and see what happens to the fourth Mrs Clements.' It wasn't until the fourth Mrs Clements was indeed found dead that a stop was put to it. When Dr Clements was told that the funeral couldn't go ahead because the police had some questions to ask him, he killed himself.

Dr John Bodkin Adams was another. Between 1946 and 1956, 160 of his patients died in suspicious circumstances, and 132 of them had left him something in their wills. People were saying, 'Isn't it a coincidence that so many of his patients die the day after they've made their will out and left all their money to him?' But he was never convicted of murder. Scandals like this should be stopped immediately, and not when everyone is dead and the truth is obvious to everyone.

I believe it's for the same reason that Mrs Bent was allowed to carry on for so long. You must not suggest that a social worker could do anything wrong. They had her registered after refusing to investigate a very serious complaint made about her.

One charity that champions patients' rights said when lobbying for this new provision to be added to the Mental Health Act: '*Any decision to do anything compulsory must be based on a wide range of evidence, including information from carers. Although this is stated in the Code of Practice, the common experience is that an assessment is still often based on a relatively short interview with the person cared for, and this can be by professionals who have never seen him/her before*'.

Suppose you pleaded with a newspaper reporter not to publish something about yourself and he replied, 'It will be all right, you can sue me for libel after it's appeared.' You would say 'I don't want to win a libel action against you, I want to not be libelled in the first place!' And suppose the editor took his side and told him not to write the article and he said, 'It'll be all right. I'll write the piece, and then you can sack me.' It would never happen.

Elizabeth's friend Madeleine complained, 'You are not to talk about having to wait 10 to 21 days for a tribunal to come round as though it's only a short time.' And instead of writing back and explaining how a patient wouldn't have to wait at all, that they'd make certain she was found not guilty before admission, not after, they wrote and said: *'We know that patients detained under the Mental Health Act have had to wait a long time for their tribunal hearings. That is why there was a recruitment campaign of further members to the tribunal, which has had some success. The situation regarding delays is now better than it was a year ago.'*

They were completely missing the point. The patient should not be there in the first place for something they didn't do.

One day I was having an 'isn't it awful' chinwag with the woman next door over the garden fence. She was hanging out the washing and still had her apron on. We were talking about mental hospitals in Britain. She said, 'It's like Russia, some of this.' I later found she had a degree in history and had done some work for Amnesty. It was an expert's opinion.

There was something we did win. The new Mental Health Act gives the patient the choice of applying to court to get their nearest relative's powers removed, if they use them unreasonably. The ministers have nothing to be frightened of from this as the mental health teams cannot be offended. Mrs Elders had wanted to leave a requirement that Elizabeth must never be in the power of her big sister, Sisley. She was told she could not do this – it was for a social worker to decide. It worried her out of her mind - what would happen to Elizabeth after she was dead? If Sisley got power, that would mean that Mrs Bent would get a share.

There are many cases of dreadful miscarriages of justice which were allowed to happen because people were afraid to challenge someone in authority who was either mistaken or dishonest. Look at the tragic case of Sally Clark. She was a solicitor who was wrongly convicted for killing two of her babies. Yet she didn't have a drink problem until after her first child died. Then she lost the second baby so they sent her to prison. It came out in court that sometimes she drank. That might have prejudiced the jury. Would they understand that the baby didn't die because she was drinking, she was drinking because the baby died?

The court was presented with statistics that suggested it had to be murder, because there was only one chance in 73 million of two cot deaths in the same family. That argument was later exposed as complete nonsense, but the paediatrician who made the claim, Professor Sir Roy Meadow, was so eminent that the court accepted it. His statement that 'One sudden infant death is a tragedy, two is suspicious and three is murder, until proved otherwise' became known as Meadow's Law, but it was later discredited.

It was a very sad case. They found out too late that she hadn't murdered them. The damage had been done; she had spent more than three years in prison and was a nervous wreck by the time they let her out. She never got over the loss of her children or the trauma of being accused of murder, and died from alcohol poisoning in 2007.

If they drive you to a nervous breakdown, they will have more power than ever. Mrs Elders would say to Mrs Bent, 'If you drive my daughter to suicide, I will never forgive you', but she couldn't have said a worse thing. It allowed them to claim Elizabeth was a suicide risk - her nearest relative had expressed concern about it, so it was their duty to take care of her. And of course, if their 'care' does drive someone to suicide, they will say, 'Doesn't it show how right we were?'

I believe it's safer to let the RSPCA inside your house than Social

Services, to let them have a look if it has been reported that you are ill treating an animal. I know of someone who, over five years, had the RSPCA round three times. The reason was simply that she took in stray and sick animals. It was understandable that some people might believe she was neglecting them, but it was the opposite – they were being brought to her neglected and she was caring for them. The RSPCA checked up and immediately accepted what the vet said. But Social Services don't always accept what doctors say.

Of course there are some more encouraging stories to tell about mental health care. In one case I know of, a woman was put into a hospital under a section and when she came out she said to the postman, 'I saw your wife in town. She did look tired! She looked as if she needed a holiday - I've just had mine!' And she started talking about the local psychiatric unit and telling him he should take his wife away there for a holiday.

They had put her on a ward with people who were a good deal worse than she was. It made her realise she was not as bad as she thought she was. A neighbour had a phone call from her and was told, 'I'll have some stories to tell you when I get back, it's mad in here!'

Yet quite a few people still thought she was 'mad'. In fact some of them weren't all that happy to see her back so soon. It depends what your standards are. Please remember that what the neighbours call an absolute riot a psychiatrist will call a spot of trouble.

The police are often very sensible in their attitudes towards people who have possible mental illness. I know of cases in which officers were well aware that people with mental health problems could be vulnerable and responded appropriately, by giving them the benefit of the doubt.

My solicitor was very satisfied with the social workers in Dover and Gorsedale, those who simply said to us 'As long as you know where we are when you need us.'

145

So some of them can get it right. But we need to be able to feel safe and secure in a society where ALL the carers get it right – or at least, as many of them as possibly can do. After all, nobody's perfect.

THE END